AVERAGE ★ ★ CIVIL ★ ★ EMPLOYEE

A NOVEL OF BUREAUCRATIC ABSURDITIES

STEPHEN J. WALLACE

RIVER GROVE
BOOKS

Published by River Grove Books
Austin, TX
www.rivergrovebooks.com

Distributed by River Grove Books

Design and composition by Greenleaf Book Group
Cover design by Greenleaf Book Group
Cover images used under license from ©Adobestock.com

Publisher's Cataloging-in-Publication data is available.

Print ISBN: 979-8-90052-035-3

eBook ISBN: 979-8-90052-036-0

First Edition

Finder's Note

On my way into work one morning, I had the great fortune of finding this manuscript. I was sitting on the Orange Line metro train when I looked down and spotted a notebook under the seats. The cover had several footprints on it, so I assumed it had been there a while, blending in with the other, mostly small pieces of morning trash on the train. I had forgotten my headphones and couldn't listen to any podcast, so I started reading the notebook. I found it surprisingly insightful and not unlike my own experience in the government, which I'd been trying unsuccessfully to put into words for a while, so I decided to share it with the world.

I am sure that Ace, whoever he is, won't mind.

—Stephen J. Wallace

1

The Start

My real name? That doesn't matter. Think of me as your Average Civil Employee. For brevity, let's do the bureaucratic thing and use an acronym: Just call me ACE—though from now on, I won't write it in all caps so it doesn't "sound" like I'm yelling my name. "Ace" implies greatness at something and certainly makes me seem more important than I really am. But I *did* survive all the executive orders, downsizing, reductions in force, government shutdowns, letting people go, calling them back, and letting them go again, at least for now—so that must count for something if I'm still here. In fact, everyone in my whole office is still here. I think the efficiency powers that be just found bigger fish to fry (and bigger offices to harass).

I work in an average cubicle in an average common area in an average building in an average—oops, "very important"—federal agency doing the people's work with grit and determination. I need to remind myself of that occasionally.

This is the first time I have ever kept a journal, but it is required now, and I got trapped into doing this because I pretended to care. A word of caution: This journal is only for me (and maybe the efficiency guru assigned to our agency), so it contains my unfiltered thoughts and some quirky nicknames to hide the real culprits. But if I ever misplace it and someone finds it and is easily offended, they should probably stop reading now and burn it. Yes, I'm talking to you—so if you keep reading, you've been warned.

Okay, here we go.

This morning, I was staring at my computer screen, and out of the corner of my eye, I saw her standing at the opening of my cube. Within this journal, I will politely refer to her as Mini. My friend NuPol came up with that name; he says she is like a minion to her mentor, though she is definitely not like the cute little yellow things in the movies. Mini is pretty much the opposite of anything cute, or little.

I glanced up. "Mini, how are you?"

"Did you hear what's happening?" she asked, her eyes wide. "As part of this whole efficiency BS, they're sending the boss to some kind of training program. He'll be gone for weeks! Meanwhile, we'll be here working like dogs."

"Well, Mini, if he's away, maybe he won't notice if we're *not* working like dogs."

Mini had to think for a minute. I thought I'd found the trick to cutting the conversation short, but I underestimated Mini's ability to get upset, even about something in her favor.

"Blah, blah, blah—unfair, blah, blah, blah—we'll get screwed, blah, blah, blah," Mini said, droning on while my mind wandered to what the special in the cafeteria might be today, what had happened to that gazelle I saw being chased on TV last night when I fell asleep, and whether I had forgotten to get my shirts out of the dryer before work. She finally stopped talking, and I searched to remember the last phrase she said. Oh, there it was, a question: "What big new bright ideas will he come back with?" She'd swayed back and forth while muttering the last three words.

"Maybe the changes will be good," I said, not trying to defend management but just trying to escape.

She scowled. "Well, wait until *she* finds out about this." Mini's eyebrows raised on "*she*."

I knew who *she* was. *She* was Mini's alpha and omega—her everything. Mini was a follower, though she could follow only one person.

Mini waited a moment, perhaps for me to shiver in fear at the thought of what *she* would do, but when I didn't, the minion slinked out of my cubicle to go enlighten someone else.

2

My Friend NuPol: The Loophole King

NuPol passed by my cubicle two minutes after Mini left. He stood at the doorway and rubbed his hands together with a sinister look on his face.

"Fresh meat on the way," he said, departing with a laugh as menacing as his look. I kind of feel sorry for the poor idiot who will be coming in to take over for our supervisor.

NuPol, which is short for New Policy, is the closest friend that I have at work. When we first met, and he found out my wife, Reima, was Latina, he referred to me as "Grispanic." I wasn't sure what he meant, but I still didn't like it much. He later explained that because I was a gringo, he wondered if I secretly wanted to be Hispanic, hence the hybrid name. After that initial bump in *el camino*, we got along well.

NuPol has the extraordinary gift of being able to find loopholes in any corporate policy. That seems to be his greatest pleasure. And once he exploits it, our organization, like any other one, then changes the policy for everyone—making it more restrictive and proactively taking away privileges having nothing to do with NuPol's original violation. I heard that he's single-handedly responsible for employing four attorneys at our agency. I thought that if management got rid of anybody during the efficiency downsizing phase, it would be him. But they seemed to only dismiss people who were actually doing something. Apparently, the new administration assumed anything done before they arrived was bad, so only those of us who don't do much are left. And besides, NuPol has figured out how to deflect blame better than anyone.

Our supervisor—or, as NuPol says, our "less-than-super-visor" (I'll just call him "Less")—is tight with the attorneys in the Office of General Counsel. This is likely because Less gets to work with them frequently because of NuPol. Less has been trying (dying, actually) to get rid of NuPol for years. Every time NuPol finds a new loophole to exploit, Less gets called into his supervisor's office and asked why he can't control his employee. Less then explains how NuPol always finds a way to show that what he did was technically *not* wrong. Then our supervisor's supervisor (or I'll call him "More of Less") writes Less up for not properly supervising his people, Less gets sent to training, and NuPol doesn't get written up for anything.

Two months ago, Less and his favorite attorney apparently felt they had NuPol dead to rights, doing personal things on a government computer, which is against policy. I had gone to Less's office to discuss an unrelated memo and, through the cracked-open door, heard Less talking on speakerphone. I raised my curled index finger to knock gently but heard voices and hesitated.

"Is this about NuPol?" I heard the attorney ask, probably since that's all Less ever calls about.

"Yep, we got him this time," Less said. "IT called. NuPol was looking at lottery results on his computer. This time, baby, it's NWO." That means "no way out." Less loves to say crap like that when he has flashes of confidence.

"I'll be right over," the attorney said.

They chatted for another minute about whether they would toast at happy hour later that day with a buttery Chardonnay from Monterey or a bold Cabernet from Washington state after security escorted NuPol out of the building. I walked away without knocking.

Employees are allowed to bring one person with them when they are called into a supervisor's office for formal counseling, and NuPol always drags me along, I guess so I can witness his brilliance. So when they called NuPol into Less's office shortly thereafter, true to form, he swung by my cube and grabbed me by the arm, almost giddy. "We have to go to the principal's office again," he said.

In Less's office, NuPol sat his lanky frame down in a guest chair and leaned his elbow over the adjacent one. I grabbed a raggedy chair with worn green fabric and foam coming out of the holes. NuPol didn't seem the least bit alarmed at the presence of the lawyer. This was an every-few-weeks affair.

"NuPol, you may wonder why we called you in here," Less said, "and why Mr. Attorney is here."

"Not really," NuPol replied, looking at his nails on his curled fingers.

"We have evidence from the CIO that you were looking at lottery results on your computer. As you remember from IT security training, it's a violation to use government computers for personal use." Less stroked his thinning black hair, smirked, and leaned back in his chair, folding his arms and putting his foot against the edge of the desk.

"I never took the IT training, so no, I didn't officially know that," NuPol said calmly, looking up and out the window as though he was just thinking aloud and not really talking to anyone.

Less took his foot off the desk and leaned forward. A slight look of concern started to creep into his countenance. "But you were supposed to take the training."

NuPol exhaled with a sound of boredom. "No, I wasn't. Don't you remember? I have a rare form of attention deficit disorder— so rare they can't even diagnose it as attention deficit disorder because I can't concentrate long enough to make the appointment to go see the doctor to get it diagnosed. Surely you remember the emails back and forth on that? It's all in my file."

Less dropped his head, but Mr. Attorney seemed to have another trick up his sleeve. "Employees have general knowledge they are not to use government equipment for personal use. This general knowledge is available from the verbal description that you received during your orientation, and everyone gets that. You are held accountable for information you receive through general knowledge, not just what you are specifically trained on. I mean, come on, you can't be trained on everything. Everybody knows you are not supposed to walk around here naked, but we never specifically tell you that."

Less raised his head again and started smiling. Knowing the way Less thinks, he figured since it came from a lawyer, it had to be right. Yes, they would get rid of NuPol because he violated what he should have known based on general knowledge.

But they underestimated NuPol. There were a million ways he could go with this: how his condition prevented him from understanding the concept of general knowledge, or how he didn't attend orientation because the room was never at the appropriate humidity for his sensitive skin, so attending could've traumatized him, forcing him to file a workers' compensation claim. However, he must have decided to save those replies for future use, probably for later when he decided to walk around the office naked. In that moment, he stoically replied, "I didn't do anything wrong."

Mr. Attorney crinkled his brow with a puzzled look. "What do you mean you didn't do anything wrong? You were looking at lottery results on your computer."

"Yes, but that was work related."

Mr. Attorney's face reddened, and his volume rose. "How the hell was that work related?"

Like a predator salivating as he moved in to kill his dinner, NuPol slowly turned his head, owllike, toward the attorney and finally made eye contact. "Because if I won the lottery, I was going to tender my resignation. Since the policy says we must be allowed to draft and submit our resignation on agency time, this would be an antecedent for my resignation and is therefore work related. You wouldn't want me to violate policy now, would you?"

Both Mr. Attorney and Less sank back in their chairs, deflated like balloons at a dart contest. I saw the redness disappear from Mr. Attorney's jowls like he was hooked up to a vacuum pump.

"Is that all?" NuPol asked, rising and walking out without waiting for an answer.

"That's all," Less obligatorily whispered.

I didn't know whether to leave or not, so I froze for a moment as I felt my eyes widen.

Mr. Attorney's head was still, but his eyes drifted toward Less. "Well, that was another waste of time." Less nodded as the lawyer walked out the door. Less bowed his head again, and I heard him mumbling; it sounded like he was praying that NuPol would win the lottery. I slinked out, hoping Less wouldn't notice me.

I understand Mr. Attorney has been working on a policy for the last three weeks that specifically says that you cannot look at lottery results on agency computers, even if you plan to retire as a result.

3

Less of Less

This journal is taking much more time than I thought it would, and part of me wants to give it up. But I know I can't, and I guess now is a good time to remind myself why I'm even keeping this strange journal with its quirky names.

During my last in-person performance appraisal (which is being updated as a new administration directive to "help our performance," though everyone knows it will just make us easier to fire), I snapped at Less. I'm not sure why exactly, but it probably had something to do with needing to completely redo my self-assessment from scratch. See, normally, I just copy my self-appraisal from the previous year and call it a day. But with this new stupid process, I have to rewrite my appraisal and stretch the truth by giving all the reasons I think this stupid new process is valuable. That, coupled with hunger pangs and the sound of my stomach growling, probably made me snap.

When Less and I discussed my self-appraisal, and we got to the new question about rating our efficiency, I made a huge mistake: I told the truth. I told Less that I didn't think I could rate myself very high. When he asked me why, I got nervous and surprised even myself when I complained about how hard it was to accomplish even simple things in our organization anymore, especially since they made it "more efficient." (I actually used air quotes.) In fact, the bureaucracy is even worse now because everyone is afraid to do anything that could get them on the naughty list.

Less looked at the notepad on his desk and let out a couple of "uh-huhs" that led me to believe he really didn't care, which I appreciated. But sadly, he did care. About twenty minutes later, when I was back at my desk, I got a call from the new Efficiency Guru in our agency. The person on the phone, whom I will just call Effing G for short, was stern and told me that he heard about the results of my performance appraisal and wanted to meet with me—immediately—in his office on the seventh floor. Now I was concerned—and a little upset. Didn't Less understand that I'd blurted out the truth in a moment of weakness? I didn't want him to really do anything. I thought he knew how this worked.

I moseyed into Effing G's pristine office, with its beige walls, an executive desk, a cherrywood-colored round table nicer than anything in our office, and a poster on the wall that said, "All things are possible." (NuPol loves these posters and loves to make new ones, like "Only believe all things are possible. Oh, and stop thinking. If you think about it, you will realize that there are very few things you can actually accomplish." They stopped putting the motivational posters up in my office because NuPol would quickly replace them with his own versions.)

Behind the square monitor of a laptop screen on the table, I saw the head of a blond guy with round glasses who mechanically said, "Sit down," without looking up or missing a keystroke. I was sure he was about twelve, though he could have been younger, and he wore a too-large blue blazer over his white T-shirt. Enough of his leg was sticking out from under the table that I could see his faded blue jeans with a hole at the knee and brown cloth loafers at the ends of his bony legs. He wore no socks, which matched his wealthy, trust-fund, youthful look that said, "I don't care, but you better."

I stood frozen until he stopped typing and, without looking up, said more forcefully, "*Sit down!*" I lunged onto the seat across the table from him, almost missing it but catching enough cheek to land. He stopped typing at the *thud* of the chair and the bump of the table. He leaned to the side and peered from behind his laptop screen, pulling his multicolored round glasses down to the end of his nose in an "I don't believe what I am seeing" gesture as he glared at me.

I felt and heard myself gulp.

"I understand you don't feel like you're accomplishing anything in this new, efficient system we've designed." He reached over to the executive desk and grabbed another laptop, barely able to hold it with his bony arm. He opened it and slid it in front of me. "Here, fill this out."

Oh, no, I thought. *I should never have been honest.* I should have said I am busy *all* the time, even after these efficiency measures have brought any real work to a halt. I skimmed the information on the screen, and it looked like a series of numbered questions. I scanned for words like "fired," "released," "resign," or "early retirement" but didn't see them.

"What is this?" I asked, hoping to sound curious rather than concerned.

Effing G went back to typing and looking at his screen. He sighed loudly and then spoke. "We care about employees who feel confused by all the changes in the government, especially since a judge in South Dakota court ordered us to care more. We need to implement steps to help you." He then tried hard to smile, which looked scarier than his earlier somber look. I guess the court order also told him he should smile. He looked back at his laptop.

"First, we need to do a screening to determine the root cause of your problem; then we do an intervention."

An intervention? That sounded even scarier than his smile looked.

I looked at the online form and started filling in my information. Below my name, department, and badge number was a checklist with fifteen numbered lines, each with a question followed by three boxes that read, "Yes," "No," or "Uncomfortable Answering." The first few questions asked me if I got enough sleep, had effective bowel movements, and was satisfied with my sex life, and then they got progressively more personal. I wasn't comfortable answering any of these questions but felt that checking that box for all of them would only prolong this torture.

After I finished, I handed the laptop back to Effing G. He pushed up his glasses and tilted his head. I felt myself gulp again, only louder.

"Oh, there is one additional question, but you have to fill it out on a different form per the injunction protocol. It can't be with the rest." He reached onto the desk again and grabbed an old clipboard with a bulky silver metal clip at the top that held down a stack of papers. A long piece of yarn was attached, and the end wrapped around a green plastic pen. "There's just one question on here, and don't write your name or any identifier."

He handed the clipboard to me. I read the question once silently and then couldn't help but read it out loud. "Do you ever have suicidal thoughts?"

I hesitated for a minute and then said, "Not until I came in here." I was mostly joking, trying to lighten the mood, but he didn't seem amused. I marked "No" and handed him the clipboard. He stared at it and then looked over his glasses without moving his head. The mood definitely wasn't lightened.

He flipped the first page over and handed the clipboard back to me. There was a different form with a lot of words. "Here, sign this."

"What is it?" I asked.

"A consent to take the screening you just completed."

"Oh," I said, very relieved. I signed it and slid the clipboard back to him.

"And consent for your intervention," he added, holding my signed form.

"Uh . . ." I started to mention that I had not read that part, but he held up a finger as if to say, "Stop." He pressed a button on the laptop and started reading from the screen.

"The protocol says you have issues with feeling productive and grateful, so we need to put you on a two-point plan. You will need to do community service and keep a detailed journal. Pause and smile."

I don't think he meant to say that last sentence from his script aloud. I was relieved that although he paused, he didn't bother forcing a creepy smile again.

He did pause for a moment and then kept reading as if nothing happened. "We will meet occasionally to discuss your progress and steps toward becoming more efficient, and we may use segments from your journal as leading indicators of how you are feeling about yourself and your work. If you don't make sufficient progress, the administration's new process states that I will need to refer you for an additional fitness-for-duty assessment." He cleared his throat just before the word "assessment," which I took to mean that the assessment would be grounds for my dismissal.

I wanted to nip this in the bud. "Uh, listen, what I said in my appraisal . . . I was just having a bad day. I'm not bothered that I don't get much done; that just seems to be the way my organization works. I really don't think I need community service or a journal."

"Your screening indicates that you need an intervention, and we would like to try this approach. Community service and a journal will help you express yourself in moments of helplessness."

I crossed my arms. "But I don't feel helpless. I was just commenting on how little my group gets done with all these changes." I straightened up, as much as I could in the chair, and boldly said, "I don't want to do this. I just want to be left alone."

He cleared his throat, louder this time, and I saw an even more menacing smile than before. "You should have thought of that before you signed. This is now part of your permanent record and will be a component of your next appraisal. If you want to keep your position, you will participate in these activities, for your own good."

I uncrossed my arms, since he'd deflated my "I'm not helpless" pose.

He warned me to diligently keep the journal and said he had the right to review it anytime, though he also added that he had a lot of cases, which I took to mean that he could review my journal but probably wouldn't. I guess this man-child had become my efficiency coach *and* therapist.

"That's all," he said.

I sat for a moment, not sure what to say. *A journal?* I thought. Who keeps a journal to help them be more gratefully efficient? I decided to be a pain in the ass so hopefully he would remove this requirement. "But I've never kept a journal. I don't know what to say," I offered as I rose out of the chair.

Again, without looking up, he said, "Just record your thoughts, both at work and at home. What you say is not as important as saying something and showing progress toward being more grateful for our new efficiency process."

Realizing I wasn't going to change his mind, I turned and started walking out. Just as I opened the door, I bumped into the next victim, who seemed to be shaking and was flipping a pill into his mouth.

I'd instinctively thanked the efficiency guru and closed the door behind me. I'd started that day complaining I was not accomplishing enough, and now I had tasks that were supposed to make me feel less helpless by apparently making me more helpless.

I guess I did need a journal.

Anyway, back to the moment at hand. Within a minute of NuPol leaving my cube (but leaving behind the echo of his sinister laugh), Buzz popped in. "Buzz" is a variation of "Bus," which is short for "Busy." His buzz haircut helps reinforce the nickname, and he likes to point at his noggin and remind people he was in the military for six months, though he never says why he was there such a short time or why he left. He must be the hardest-working person I know. Buzz has so much going on that sometimes he sits in my cubicle for hours on end telling me how busy he is. Once, I removed my guest chair, but that didn't deter old Buzz. He went to the empty cube next to mine and brought in *two* chairs, resulting in spots for even more guests to invade my space.

I sometimes keep looking at my screen, pretending to work

while he talks, but Buzz continues. He has so much to do, and therefore *so* much to say, that he just keeps plowing through his myriad of assignments while I nod and occasionally throw in a "really" or "sounds like a lot."

While Buzz rocked back on the rear two legs of my guest chair, babbling about how there was no way he would ever finish everything, Less appeared at the cubicle opening (I don't really have a door). I've slightly altered Buzz's following attempt at a joke so everyone can keep their assigned journal names.

"Knock, knock," Less said, tapping on the metal frame that was holding the panels of my cubicle together.

"Who's there?" Buzz asked and then let out with a howl, apparently assuming the rest of us understood how brilliantly funny this was. When no one responded, Buzz broke into his own routine. He rested the chair on all fours and leaned to one side as the chair squeaked.

"Less," Buzz himself answered. He leaned to the other side of the chair with a squeak, I guess trying to give the effect that he was mimicking different people. Out of the other side of his mouth, he asked, "Less who?"

He leaned again. *Squeak.* "The less you keep me waiting, the better." Buzz tilted his head back and guffawed. (I knew my word-of-the-day calendar would come in handy.)

After rolling his eyes, Less said sternly, "Funny, Buzz. I need to speak to Ace."

"Uh-oh. What'd you do now, buddy boy?" Buzz asked me. "Surfing porn again?" He rose from his chair.

I get nervous with jokes like that; even obvious jokes can offend curious listeners.

Less cleared his throat and let out what sounded like a faint growl. "Um, Ace, could you please find the latest draft of the memo on that new appointee position, print it out, and bring it to my office? We need to talk about it. I think it's on the shared drive."

Now, I must digress for a moment. I hate, hate, *hate* the stupid shared drive. My group has tried several iterations of the shared drive with no success. We tried one version where everyone was able to edit the documents at the same time and see who else was editing them. NuPol kept going online to see who was editing which document and would undo every edit in real time. A friend of his in IT must have given him overwrite permission to do it anonymously, though no one in IT ever confessed.

We then went back to an older version of the shared drive that has a bunch of subdirectories, and that's what we currently use. But this is a new battleground because now everybody has read/write privileges for subdirectory names and content, and they are always changing the names (and changing them back) so that no one—least of all me—can ever find anything. I'm really not sure why we even call them our individual drives anymore, since everyone seems to be changing everything in everyone else's subdirectory, including the name.

I always try to do things the easiest way. I simply named my subdirectory "ACE" on the shared drive, with some sub-subdirectories listed under that. However, others feel this is problematic and "help" me by "improving" my directory nomenclature, so the name changes often. In staff meetings, we used to talk about the requirement that everyone leave everyone else's directories alone, but that just seemed to make the problem worse. So we all just live with it now.

One time, Less had looked into the possibility of each person being the only one with read, write, and renaming capabilities in their own directory, but I understood that would have required him to complete more than one form, so that was never going to happen.

I hopped on the server and hunted and hunted, and just as I was ready to give up, I saw a directory called "theADirectory." Knowing my colleagues, they probably felt that made more sense than just putting my name. I clicked on it, and sure enough, there were my subdirectories. I didn't know whether to be glad I found it or terrified that I was starting to think like my coworkers.

Less was shuffling papers when I arrived at his door.

"You wanted to see me?" I asked. "I have the memo."

"Yes, Ace, come on in and have a seat. There are a couple of things we need to talk about."

The memo discussion, which I dreaded anyway, had now grown into a "couple of things." I looked around his office. He is privileged to have an office of his own, even though it is not very stylish. The small couch against the wall looks like something we used to pitch into the dumpster at the end of the semester in college. The smattering of paper all over his desk gives the impression that Less is both always working and always trying to find something to work on. The faded black-and-white print of some guy fly-fishing on the wall speaks to a bygone era, probably about forty years ago, when someone dug that print out of the garbage and hung it on Less's wall, which wasn't even his wall at the time. Occupants came and went, but the print stayed. You have to admire that.

"Ace, I know you've been working hard on this memo, but we have a problem."

I looked at the freshly printed memo.

"Go ahead and read it," Less said ominously.

"Subject: Memorandum to create the new position title for the Assistant Sub-Secretary. Background: With the recent reorganization, a new position has been created. The position resides between the Assistant Secretary and the Deputy Assistant Secretary. This new position necessitates appropriate paperwork to establish roles and responsibilities, which can then be delegated to other positions. Because of this—"

"That's enough," Less said. "Do you see a problem with this?"

I perused the page for misspellings and saw none, but I knew there must be a problem because of Less's question. "Too formal?" I offered.

"Look at the title. Assistant Sub-Secretary. Did you ever think what acronym we would use for that title?"

I resisted the temptation to point out that Less had come up with that title. I had just written the justification memo.

"Well, it does have a hyphen," I offered weakly.

Less breathed in through gritted teeth. "Well, people above me think some will be tempted to remove the hyphen, and we don't want anyone in the organization making fun of our senior leaders."

I let out an involuntary laugh because making fun of leadership is about all anyone in the organization does anymore. I pretended I was coughing as cover.

"I'm afraid you're going to have to start over, come up with a new title, and run this through the concurrence process again," Less said, calmer than he normally sounds.

"Okay, I'll get on this right away," I said, realizing that if I considered recent lessons learned from our new pretend efficiency process, I only had about two weeks to come up with a different title and six months to run it through our concurrence process requiring twelve signatures. By the time we got the title approved, the person may have left the position, and we could have a reorganization that would make the title obsolete. Even if the position stayed, history showed that the next person would want a different title anyway.

Less exhaled. "There's something else I need to talk to you about. Close the door."

Oh, no. It was one of the close-the-door talks. Usually, only NuPol gets those. In addition to helping me appreciate our new efficiency model, I was starting to appreciate that my journal could help me cope with anxious moments, but I didn't have it with me.

"You may have heard that the organization is focusing on cultivating better leadership at my level. I am going to be, uh, attending a three-month training program to improve my abilities." Less leaned back and looked at the ceiling. "I have to go," he said, throwing his worn globe squeeze ball into the air and catching it on the way down.

After what seemed like hours, he sat back up and looked at me. "There won't be any more money for the person stepping in—just the opportunity to show leadership and the satisfaction of knowing they're helping the organization."

I had to cough-cover a laugh again. So that was it. He was bringing everyone in individually to tell them who the new boss would be. Probably some up-and-comer, maybe one of those future leaders in the Secretary's office, which meant they would be about twenty-two, thinking they knew everything about management because they were class president in high school and—even better—took a business class at some college I didn't even feel worthy to pronounce. They probably wore sweaters with emblems all the time—even in summer. I was sure that this group would humble them, the poor bastard.

Less continued. "We don't have it in the budget to pick up someone from outside our department. I thought about who is already here that I could leave in charge for the next three months. I, uh, ruled out NuPol, Buzz, Mini, and, of course, *her*—for obvious reasons—so that really just leaves me with you."

Oh, no, I thought as I felt every single cell in my body gasp. *Where the hell is my journal?*

4

The Announcement

Setting: Drab conference room. Interior of a dilapidated old building in Washington, DC.

Cast: Less (the supervisor), NuPol, Mini, Buzz, and me (Ace).

Scene: Less sits at the head of the table. He prefers that seat, but when NuPol gets there first, he always jumps to the head of the table, knowing he will never be asked to move. Less has started getting there about twenty minutes early so he can beat NuPol to his spot.

"Okay, all, we have a couple of things to talk about today," Less started.

"I didn't see an agenda. You know how that triggers me," NuPol said.

Less sighed. "NuPol, we couldn't create an agenda because in the last meeting, you said seeing an agenda in advance triggers you and gives you anxiety. Don't you remember?" I used to dismiss

NuPol and his constant anxieties, but after my talk with Less, I can definitely sympathize with him more.

"Bringing up my past traumas triggers me too," NuPol said, rubbing his temples.

"Okay, no more talking about past traumas, agendas, or triggers," Less said, more assertive than he usually sounded.

NuPol drew in a breath like he was going to talk, but Less jumped in.

"I have one bit of business to address from our last meeting. As we discussed before, because of the judge's order reversing the reversing of the diversity initiatives, we again want to promote inclusion in every sense. That means giving chances to people who are disabled, er . . . uh . . ." Less looked down at his notepad and corrected himself. "Otherly abled." Less made finger quotes at those two words.

Less continued. "The only disabled person—I mean, otherly abled person—that we had in the department was recently reassigned to be the Director of the Office of Outreach to Disabled Individuals and Employees, or OODIE. So they have chosen our office to provide a representative from the community of the otherly abled."

"Wait," Mini said, "I thought we weren't supposed to say disabled. The name of the office includes the word 'disabled.'"

Less exhaled loudly. "It doesn't make a good acronym if we call it the Office of Outreach to Otherly Abled Employees. OOOAE doesn't roll off the tongue. But if we use the word 'disabled,' we can say OODIE. Like 'Foodie' but without the 'F.' Besides, the disabled—I mean, otherly abled—woman who is the director came up with that name, so it's okay for the rest of us to say it. But only when we are talking about the name of the office."

NuPol jumped in. "How are you saying this with a straight face?"

Less ignored him and continued. "The problem is now we have no otherly abled employees for her to reach out to."

"I remember this conversation now," NuPol chimed in again. "You want one of us to become disabled so we'll make the quota."

Less shook his index finger in a back-and-forth motion. "Not at all. I am just encouraging you that, if you already have a disability and did not feel comfortable declaring it before, you are in a safe space to declare it now."

"Here, in front of everyone else? This is the safe space?" Mini asked, voice raised.

Less scratched his temple, and I thought I saw a trickle of sweat. "Well, this *is* a safe space."

Buzz rocked forward in his chair. "You remember I told you about my cousin who works at the Papa John's in Falls Church? She walks with a limp."

Less grabbed his pen and started scribbling in his notepad. He enthusiastically said, "Yes, I do remember. I told you we could rewrite the description for the new analyst position so that anyone can do it. Nobody knows what an analyst does here anymore anyway. Maybe at least we can bring her in as an intern."

Buzz nodded. "Well, she started going to physical therapy, so she might be able to walk without a limp soon."

"Shit," Less said and then cleared his throat. "I mean, good. But if it doesn't take, get back to me. In the meantime, if any of you happen to remember a disability that you have and want to disclose it, don't hesitate. And if you happen to fall or anything . . ." Less briefly paused to air quote "fall or anything" before continuing. "Like, if you then need special help, maybe we could get a favorable ruling. We only have a few weeks left to come up with someone."

"My God," Mini mumbled under her breath.

Less turned the page on his notepad. "Okay, moving on to the last item on the agenda." He paused and looked at NuPol, who just smiled. "As you may have heard, the organization is investing more in its people because people are our greatest asset."

"Bullshit," NuPol said, pretending to cough, reminiscent of a scene from the movie *Animal House*. Less ignored him again.

"Well, that commitment also extends to supervisors. The organization feels it is good to make sure supervisors like me have the best training so that I can better guide and coach each of you to be successful, which obviously means more efficient."

I scanned the faces around the table and saw multiple eye rolls. I think everyone is sick of hearing the word "efficient."

"Sending you to charm school, huh?" NuPol said, snickering.

This time, Less could not let it go.

"This is not *charm* school! They want to make sure I'm cultivating the skills that will allow me to guide each of you to your full potential." He looked straight at NuPol. "It's easier to guide some of you than others."

"Look, Less, we've heard all this," NuPol said. "Haven't you noticed that we all sit in a cubicle farm and hear every word that's said? Just tell us who they're sending over here from the Secretary's office to replace you so we can get started with the initiation."

I had been in a stupor since leaving Less's office earlier. I didn't even remember telling him that I would take the role, not that I had a choice. The world had felt hazy as I'd walked back to my cube and reached for my black binder that I make notes in during all our staff meetings. (Truth is, I only make notes to stay awake. I never look back at them.) NuPol's frank admission about hazing the newcomer and the impending announcement of my sentence shook me out of the fog.

Less half smiled. "Well, that's part of the good news. It won't be someone from the Secretary's office. The organization has seen fit to give this great opportunity to someone from our own team—someone who knows our group best."

"Couldn't pony up the money from your budget to bring someone in from outside, eh?" NuPol seemed to say out loud and to himself at the same time.

"Your new supervisor for the next three months will be our very own Ace."

I didn't look up, but I could hear the gasps. When I finally did lift my head, I saw NuPol giving me the same sinister glare he had flashed in my cubicle earlier.

I knew this wasn't the last time I would hear the gasps or see NuPol's glare. This was going to be a long three months.

5

Community Disservice: Part I

The Washington, DC, chapter of my alma mater, South Central Missouri State, meets at a bar in northern Virginia during football and basketball seasons to watch games. I attend about five games a year. While I like our team and want to be supportive, we are not very good and almost never win, but I go occasionally to keep some connection to the school and generally because I don't have anything else to do. Since South Central Missouri State is not one of the big players in college sports, we command a very small part of the bar. Our alumni association is dominated by a few people who always get there early and save the few available seats for their friends. I mostly just stand in the corner wondering why I came.

Another reason I don't go often is that I feel humiliated, not only because we always lose but also because of our mascot. Our mascot, for some strange reason, is a pigeon. We are known as the South Central Pigeons. Now, I kind of like pigeons, but I'm not sure it's the best mascot. When I was in school, I used to occasionally hear people on campus say that we'd lost another game, probably because the opponent felt emboldened that we had such a chicken shit mascot. (Or perhaps I should say "pigeon shit" in this case.)

The person who was in the mascot outfit, at least when I was there, didn't help matters. Our pigeon would bend over at the waist and pretend to eat food off the field. It would occasionally look up and jerk its head from one side to the other. While everyone agreed it really did act like a pigeon, this behavior definitely did not invoke fear in the hearts of our opponents. In fact, I remember one time, the opposing mascot, which was a wildcat, started laughing so hard at our pigeon that the wildcat lost its head. Literally. It jerked its head back, and the artificial wildcat head came off. The person beneath, who appeared to be a guy, was laughing and rubbing his eyes with his big fake cat paws. And the more he laughed, the more our mascot walked around the field, kicking one foot at a time behind him, bent at the waist, pretending to eat food off the field.

Our school definitely would have won the prize (if there had been one) for the mascot with the most dexterity and whose actions were most authentically like its namesake, but we won very little else. I later heard a rumor that the mascot during my time was the football coach's son and that he also liked to do impressionistic dance or something like that. His dad was probably too busy paying attention to what was happening with our pitiful team to notice what a laughingstock our mascot was, but that would explain why the pigeon kept his job. Even now, I can't see our mascot on TV without feeling embarrassed for our whole school.

Anyway, I'd volunteered to spearhead the alumni charity activity. I don't like even admitting that I'm on my school's alumni board, but I am this year, through no fault of my own. It is another assignment I was roped into by a sometimes-game-watch friend. I was terrified of running the event. In fact, I'd almost backed out because I was sure I would do something to invoke the ire of the head of the local chapter of the alumni association. Now let me tell you about this head, whom I consider Alumna Extraordinaire. I'll just drop some of the letters and call her Alex for short. Seeing the way Alex runs the organization, one would assume it is her whole life. She reminds me of the diligence of another woman who used to run the homeowners' association in the condo community where Reima and I live in Arlington, just outside DC.

That woman, homeowner lady—I'll just call her HO—had cared deeply about making sure that everything was done in accordance with all the chapters and verses of the 379-page homeowner's policy. We'd felt her wrath one time when we had a particularly full bag of trash. Our compactor could compact it no more, and our normal pickup time was Saturday between 1:00 p.m. and 3:00 p.m. Reima and I were going to be out after 11:30 a.m., so I dared to take our trash out a bit early—at 11:29 a.m. But I was very clever. I snuck down the block and put the trash on the corner where multiple condo owners put their trash bags. I was sure there was no way it could ever be traced back to us. However, when we returned to the house around 3:30 p.m., HO was standing at our front door, tapping her foot. I approached with caution, but I was sure we had covered our trash tracks sufficiently, so I showed no fear.

"Hi, HO. How are you?"

"Are you Ace?" she asked with a stoic expression.

My boldness was slipping away. "Uh, yes."

"You know the rules about the trash. You put yours out too early."

I decided to feign ignorance.

"Whatever do you mean, HO?"

"I know that your trash bag was at the corner *well* before 1:00 p.m. We don't like it when people flaunt our rules. We would all live in chaos if everyone acted like you."

"But how do you know it was me?" I heard both confusion and fear in my voice.

"I noticed there was one more bag on the corner than we would expect, given the average rate of trash we generally observe. I went through every one of those bags and found an envelope with your address from the power company. By the way, you should have recycled that."

I was caught dead to rights. Not only had I put my trash out early, but my sinister ploy to place it alongside bags that were legitimately there was exposed. And I had violated the beloved recycle policy.

Then Reima, who had been observing from a distance, walked up and started speaking Spanish. HO tried to explain the home-owner's policy in painfully slow English, but Reima kept saying, "No entiendo."

HO finally got frustrated and started walking away. I guess the joys of enforcing compliance with the sacred homeowner's policy lose their luster when you have to do it in another language, at least for HO.

We slinked inside like wounded boxers who had survived the round but knew they would lose the match. We watched her from our front window as she walked away and turned around every few steps to talk and wag her finger at us, even though we were in our townhouse. Reima looked at me. "Idiot, I told you not to mess with her. Why didn't you just wait to put the trash out? She'll put us on the naughty list. I've seen this happen in Colombia. We never get off!" Then I heard story after story about how bad it was when people showed up at the door in her home country to take people away. She followed me from room to room enlightening me. After about half an hour of hearing "and another time," she'd finally stopped with the examples. Of course, she'd been right, as always. No authority—from cartels to the police—could hold a grudge like HO. I'd walked to the window and looked out the front door, hoping the police would show up so I could voluntarily surrender.

6

Community Disservice: Part II

So back to the story of my community service. I was driving to the alumni board meeting just after Effing G had put me on an efficiency intervention. I had started keeping this journal but still wasn't sure how to do something charity-wise to check my box. But as luck would have it, I passed a church with a large dumpster-looking container in the parking lot. The sign on the receptacle read, "Donate clothes here for the less fortunate."

So when the head Alumna Extraordinaire, Alex, announced at the meeting that they were looking for a volunteer to spearhead the charity event—which some freshman back at the university had brilliantly decided would have the theme "Not Just for Pigeons"—I had a great idea. I would volunteer to collect clothes and bring them to the church dumpster. This, I figured, would be easy. I would just ask people to bring their "gently used" clothes to the football game the day of the charity drive, and I would collect them and drop them off. Easy peasy; nothing could go wrong.

When I jumped in and suggested this at our meeting, Alex and one of her lap dogs, a mousy, diminutive guy with slicked-back thinning black hair who I'll refer to as Little Alex #1, seemed to scoff at my suggestion.

"Hmmmm," was all Alex had to say.

"I don't know," said Little Alex #1. "This is an important tradition, and the weight and reputation of the entire chapter are riding on successfully pulling off this charity event."

I swallowed hard. "I know, but I want to get involved, and I really want to help the less fortunate." *And I really want to check the box for my community service*, I thought. Now, it may sound like my intentions were less than honorable, but the way I see it, it was a win-win. I help do some good, which I almost never do, and the alumni group benefits. Oh, and the less fortunate benefit too—I can't forget them. Alex finally consented to let me try my idea, though it was apparently at great risk to the reputation of the entire university.

When I'd gleefully emailed Effing G about the arrangement, he'd simply responded with "Fine" and reminded me that I needed to get the chapter leader to sign off (literally—Alex had to sign a paper—must be a Silicon Valley thing) that I had fulfilled my duty at the charity event. I should have known it had to be documented because there was no way he could trust me.

So the day of the charity drive arrived. The university always sent a token of appreciation to everyone in any of the seventeen chapters across the country who participated in the event. Last year, the gifts were South Central Pigeon frames for license plates, and the year before that, they sent flags. (I know because Alex sent an email around letting the nonparticipating members of the chapter know what they'd missed.) This year, they were supposed to send the token gifts to my house, but nothing had arrived yet, and I was getting a bit nervous. The last thing I needed was to go to the game that night and tell Alex that I didn't have the participation gifts.

Much to my relief, when I got home from work, there was a big box on my front steps. Unless Reima had ordered something from Amazon, this was it. I looked at the mailing label: from Missouri. *Bingo!* The gifts had arrived.

I glanced at my watch. *Shit.* With all the chaos, I had lost track of time. I grabbed the box and headed to the community garage five blocks away, where I keep my truck. You see, in residential areas outside DC, there are often too many townhouses and too little street parking. We are supposed to get one space per townhouse, but unfortunately, my neighbor, or I should say "neighbors," next door don't really pay much attention to that allowance. They don't seem to pay attention to *any* of the so-called rules.

For instance, there is a rule that you are not supposed to sublease any part of your townhouse. When we'd first moved in, I saw no potential of anybody doing that, since the townhouses are all the same size and ours is barely big enough for me and Reima. I soon found out that not everyone sees it that way. Next to us is an end unit that I assume belongs to a goateed, pudgy, short guy who is a writer and wears colorful muscle pants (though his body suggests he should wear otherwise). He shares the townhouse with a large man whom I have determined, from the two short conversations we have had in three years, to be from South Asia, and the two men seem to be extremely close.

Apparently, the South Asian man's family—a wife and six kids— live in the basement, or that's what I picked up from talking to the wife for a couple of minutes as we stood in front of our houses watching the meager July Fourth parade last year. I asked her how they were connected to the colorful-muscle-pants guy who owned the house. She raised her eyebrow, held her head still but looked to the right and then back to me, and said, "I guess you could say he's like a, uh, brother to my husband."

"Oh, that's nice," I said sincerely. "And how long have you lived here?"

I knew they'd been living there when we moved in three years before, and I had seen them going in and out of the house practically every day since then. But she replied, "We don't live here; we just visit from time to time." Before I could ask another question, she grabbed three of her children, muttered something I didn't understand, and walked them all down the block to the corner farthest away from me.

In addition to those eight people, there also seems to occasionally be other families from somewhere in Central or South America who temporarily move in and out of Muscle Pants' townhouse. It doesn't really bother me but seems to infuriate Reima. "I left South America to get away from shit like this," she mumbles every time we see any of the members of the "United Nations" coming or going next door. I'm not sure what she means, but we both learned early on that we could either fight with everyone about everything or we could just live with it and try not to let things bother us.

That's because we get caught for any little infraction while everyone else gets away with murder, but I've just figured out how to put it out of my mind. There are those who get caught and those who don't. We get caught. Reima says it's because I'm a gringo and they don't expect me to skirt the rules, so they focus on me. So much for my white privilege.

We rarely interact with our neighbors these days, but we do occasionally get the opportunity whenever Reima's family comes to visit. It's always a time of wonder whenever they arrive—usually because we're not even sure which airport they will arrive at, so despite any instructions and travel plans previously discussed, we must be ready to jump at a moment's notice and drive between an hour and the better part of a day to pick them up at the *other* airport at some random time, and I get to enjoy their loud, rambling musings in Spanish all the way home.

One time when her family visited, our nephew had been assigned a class project. He'd been allowed to come with the rest of the family to visit on the condition that he didn't fall behind in his schoolwork. I never got the story completely straight, but I think the project was supposed to be collecting native leaves or something. But I do know that Reima's father took his lead role as proxy teacher very seriously and decided it would be better to make a flower collection.

When I got home from work one day, the entire family was hunkered around the coffee table, where a poster board had several flowers taped on it. I could see the names of the flowers written in English and Spanish. Everyone was speaking calmly, so I should have suspected something was wrong.

"Reima, tell him that's a nice flower collection he has there," I offered, hoping to come across as supportive.

She looked up expressionless. "Don't answer the door."

"What? Why?" I asked. Almost immediately, the doorbell rang. I went to the front window and pulled back the curtain a crack to see who was there. It was Muscle Pants.

"It's our neighbor," I mouthed to Reima.

She held up her index finger to her lips. Then the bell turned into loud thumps.

I looked out midway through the thumps and saw that his hand had moved to a *Psycho* shower scene maneuver, but instead of stabbing a knife into someone, he seemed to be trying to kill our door with his fist.

"I've got to answer—something must be wrong," I said in a hushed tone. "I'll take care of it."

I opened the door and put on a smile; at least I hoped it came across as a smile. "Hi, neighbor. How are you?"

"Do you know anything about what happened to my flower garden?" he asked, pointing to the diagonal box that protruded out about five feet at the end wall of his unit. Just this morning it had been full of yellow and purple and red blooms. I looked over and saw blossomless stems hanging over the side as if they were crying after a terrible storm.

I knew exactly what had happened, but I pretended I didn't. "Hmm, what's wrong with it?"

His eyes widened, and he raised his voice. "What's *wrong*? Can't you see? All the flowers are gone! I want to know what happened."

His eyes moved from me to the gap between me and the door. I moved to block his view of the table with my nephew's beautiful collection inside. "Yes, now that you mention it, I think I can tell something happened to them. Wonder if an animal got in there? You know, occasionally we see deer around. I hear they eat flowers."

"It doesn't look like a deer got them," he said, moving his body to try to see what I was blocking. "It looks like somebody cut them."

I scratched my head like I was thinking. "Well, that's a shame. I'll let you know if I hear anything." He started standing on his tiptoes, trying to see over me, and then I stood on my tiptoes, too, and said, "I have to check on dinner!" before shutting the door so he couldn't say something else. "Get that board to the basement," I said sharply but just above a whisper. Reima nodded.

For some strange reason, we've just never formed a close relationship with our neighbors.

Anyway, because all the UN members next door have cars, either large ones with tinted windows or trucks bigger than the entire townhouse, complete with landscaping tools secured by ropes, we have no place for my truck. So in "go along to get along" mode, I park in the community lot five blocks away. Since I take a bus to catch a train to work, I don't need to have a car every day. It is a pain to walk to the garage when I do need my car in the evenings, but I've accepted it. When Reima and I are going somewhere, I walk to the garage by myself and drive to the townhouse to pick her up. That saves me five blocks of hearing her complain about how much we are persecuted—another variation of the "we always get caught" refrain. The neighbors have parking spaces close by, and Reima gets picked up, so this protocol seems to work out for everyone. Well, maybe except for me.

I definitely didn't want to be late to the game and incur the wrath of Alex, so I grabbed the box from Missouri and started walking briskly to my truck. The box didn't feel too heavy, so it probably wasn't the metal license plate holders again. Maybe it was a bunch of flags with our pigeon mascot on them. I reached my truck and plopped the cardboard box onto the passenger's seat. After a twenty-minute drive, I pulled into the parking lot outside the bar just as the game was about to start.

Oh, no, I thought. *The wrath of Alex is sure to come.*

I hustled out of the truck and dashed into the bar since I was running late. I could come back for the box later—maybe during a commercial.

A white-haired man with a Hawaiian shirt and captain's hat was coming out the front door of the bar as I was going in. "Hold on, sailor. What's the rush?" he asked.

"In a hurry," I said between breaths, muscling past him.

Sure enough, Alex was waiting inside, arms crossed, mouth scrunched unapprovingly to one side, tapping a foot. Her four usual lackeys stood around her in a semicircle, as if Alex were the head of a human cul-de-sac. She looked at me, looked at her watch, and then looked back at me.

"I thought you were coming earlier," she said sternly, her eyes throwing looks like javelins.

The bad-traffic excuse doesn't really work in DC, since there's always bad traffic, so I decided to play up the work "issue."

"Had an unexpected issue creep up at work I had to deal with."

I was proud of my reply until her retort, "We all have important jobs that have—how do you say—issues that creep up, but you must be dedicated to your volunteer activities as well. We depend on each other." She raised her eyebrows at the word "creep."

I felt my head bow. "It won't happen again."

She turned away from me to her second in command. "Okay, he'll make the announcement about his little charity project at the end of the first quarter. Then we'll do the raffle for the signed football at halftime. Everybody clear?" she asked with a crescendoed voice that both asked the question and let us know that there was only one answer.

I could have done without the characterization of my clothing drive as a "little charity project" but decided to ignore it. Besides, all I had to do was make my announcement, collect the clothes, and take them to the dumpster beside the church. In return, I would get my form signed. Easy peasy.

I hobbled to the corner of the bar where our alumni group was and saw a small sea of maroon and yellow jerseys with pigeons on them. The regulars had already moved seats around and packed close quarters, so I was left to stand in the corner against the wall. But I didn't care; I had only one mission tonight: clothes, dumpster, form.

"You stuck against the wall again, too?" I turned around and saw Chris, our alumni group treasurer. I had to do a double take because he looked different. He wasn't wearing his school sweatshirt as usual. Instead, he had a gray button-up shirt on his big-boned (but not fat) body.

He must have seen the look of confusion on my face. "GQ tonight. Besides, the shirt matches my salt and pepper hair. 'Course, it's more salt than pepper lately with all that's been going on at my agency."

Chris is probably the only member of the alumni group I feel any connection with. We only talk at these games, but he always seems friendly. He is the only one of Alex's lackeys on the board who seems normal. I suspect that she leaves him alone because he doesn't openly defy her, so for years he has run unopposed and has control over the club's money. He seems to be a bit of a loner and the only one (besides me) who doesn't jam a seat into the crowd around the bar tables that are only big enough for four but end up having many more on game days. He and I are also the only ones not wearing pigeon jerseys. His only sin against me is that he was the one who roped me into being on the alumni board with Alex. I have cursed him for that many times behind his back, but I suspect he did it to have another sane person around to share in Alex overload, and I really can't blame him.

"Yep, stuck by the wall again. But hey, at least we got this table beside us for our beers and wings," I said, smiling.

Chris looked at the makeshift table, a piece of plywood of about three by three feet that was supported by four high-top barstools. It's where Alex always puts posters and items for the raffles. She'd already put a framed poster on it with a picture of the coach signing the football that was going to be raffled off at halftime.

"Uh-huh . . . a 'table,'" Chris managed with a tone of both agreement and sarcasm. "You're looking a little worse for wear, too, Ace. I see more gray in your dirty-blond mane, and it looks like you've found some of the weight I'm trying to lose." He smiled.

"Yep, things are pretty hosed up at my agency, too. Guess I'm stress eating and worrying more," I replied.

We both mindlessly stared at the big-screen TV on the other side of the room. Only three minutes into the first quarter and the pigeons had already allowed three touchdowns: 21–0. "It's gonna be another ugly one," Chris said, shaking his head.

We watched a few more minutes as I awaited my chance: the end of the first quarter.

When our mascot came on the field and pretended to eat food off the turf, Chris and I looked away from the TV. I saw other pigeon fans hide their faces in their hands and shake their heads. The beloved field-eating gesture has stood the test of time.

"So tonight's your big night, huh?" Chris said.

I forced a smile. "Yes, tonight I do some good. Clothes for the less fortunate."

Chris scratched his temple and scanned the room. "Doesn't look like anyone brought any clothes. Where are they?"

I froze. *Oh, shit.* Did I send the email saying that we were collecting clothes tonight? I thought I did. Surely, I did. Right?

"Uh, do you remember getting an email from me about the clothes drive tonight?" I asked Chris.

Chris wrinkled his mouth to one side and looked upward for a moment. "Now that you mention it, I don't. I just remember you talking about it at one of our board meetings. I guess nobody outside the few of us on the board even knows about it."

I felt the blood drain from my face. How could this have happened? And if I forgot, why didn't Alex remind me? That's the kind of thing she'd delight in lording over me. She wouldn't give me the benefit of the doubt that I just forgot. She would assume I was too incompetent to do this simple task and belittle me with explicit instructions, like making sure my computer is turned on when I send it. I felt warm moisture roll down my forehead and looked her way. Alex seemed to be glaring at me, almost smiling. I'm not sure if she'd just figured out that I screwed up or had known it all along and was waiting for me to realize it. Either way, this was a great night for her and a bad night for me.

The next few minutes passed in a fog. It seemed like people were moving in slow motion. There was some action on the TV, and I thought I saw a score of 41–0, but I couldn't really hear anything. The pigeon jerseys swayed back and forth in a sea of maroon and yellow while people laughed and wiped ranch dressing and buffalo sauce off their chins. But I felt the tension swell. I imagined myself as Frankenstein's monster running in the woods and being chased toward a cliff by a mob wearing pigeon jerseys, holding chicken wings in one hand and torches in the other. Then I pictured myself in a prom dress, standing in a gym, and they've poured pig's blood on me, like in the movie *Carrie*. I could hear the haunting voice of Carrie's mother chanting, "Ace, they're all laughing at you. They're all laughing at you!"

My cinematic role-playing was suddenly stopped by a whistle on the TV and the presence of Alex in the middle of the room. "Okay, can you cut the sound?" she asked. A young guy standing in what looked like a DJ booth twisted a nob, and all was silent.

"All right, everyone. One of our, um, members, would like to make an announcement. As you may know, or probably don't know, today was supposed to be our charity event. As you remember from past years, this event is a big deal with alumni groups across the country. It is one of the most important milestones for any alumni club. This year, that effort was led by . . ." She waved her arm in my direction without even looking at me. "That guy in the corner. Ace. Let's all listen to what he has to say for himself." The last sentence sounded magnified, but maybe it was because of my stupor.

The heads on top of the pigeon jerseys all turned my way, and I could hear chairs scraping against the wooden floor as the alums turned their bar chairs toward me. Their faces seemed both void and full of disbelief. I took a couple of steps away from the wall.

"Um, like Alex said, I'm Ace. Just call me that guy in the corner." I forced a laugh. No one else did. I felt the last bit of blood in my face drain out, leaving me lightheaded. I continued. "This year, we had a great idea to help the less fortunate by donating clothes. But I, uh, think maybe there was one oversight. You see, we didn't quite get the word out, and only some of us—"

Alex held up her hands high with fingers outstretched and yelled, "Only six."

I continued. "Well, very few of us knew about it. So you may not have known that we were going to collect clothes this evening." I heard my own voice shaking. Then, I had a moment of brilliance. "Today is the last day of the charity drive, so I need to deliver the clothes tonight. So even though you didn't know about it, if you're wearing any clothes that you'd like to donate, I'll be glad to take them." There was total silence for a few seconds; you could hear a feather float.

7

Community Disservice: Finale

Then, suddenly, there was a tsunami of laughter. It seemed to grow louder with each passing second. A woman at the table closest to me started wiping tears from her hollow cheeks between guffaws. (That word-of-the-day calendar continued to pay off!) One of the older, heftier alumni men who has never been known for his tact stood up and pretended to unbuckle his belt. "Hey, son, I'll give you a pair of my underwear! Maybe they'll count as two pieces."

The young frat-looking guy sitting next to him spewed beer all over the table, and people began laughing so hard that they started to snort like pigs as they gasped for breath. The pigeons on their shirts were moving so much that they looked like a flock getting ready to take off. I glanced at Chris, who shrugged his shoulders. I realized there was no way to salvage the situation, so I just stepped backward, feeling behind me until my hand hit the wall.

After a couple of more minutes of laughter, jokes, and finger-pointing in my direction, Alex held up her hand to calm the group. "Well, now that we know never to leave Ace in charge of something, let's get back to the game. And fear not, we've always been a second-half team." The guy in the DJ booth wearing a Tupac shirt turned the knob again, and the game sound was back on. Thankfully, everyone turned back around, their eyes glued to the riveting game on TV.

"God, that was brutal," Chris said to me.

"I guess I deserved it," I said. "I was sure I sent out an email, but—" Then something caught my eye. A brown cloth was sticking out from behind a divider that separated our bar area from the kitchen. "What's that?" I pointed at the fabric.

Chris glanced toward the kitchen. "Looks like clothes. Maybe somebody did get the message after all."

I went over to the table behind the divider and looked behind the poster. There were clothes. There must have been about four or five pairs of pants, a few T-shirts, and sweatshirts.

"Chris," I said, a bit of life creeping back into my voice. "Somebody did bring clothes and left them here for me to collect. I guess they either left before I made my speech or were too scared to confess, given the mood of Alex and the crowd."

"I guess," said Chris, more as a question than agreement.

"Can you help me carry these to my truck?"

"What? And miss this barnburner of a game?" Chris asked and then smiled and grabbed a handful of shirts.

"I guess it's not a total loss," I said as we walked to the door of the bar. I heard someone yelling as we exited. Must've been a touchdown.

We were about halfway through the parking lot, and the yelling seemed to follow us.

"Oh, no," Chris said. "Don't look now, but you've drawn a crowd."

We turned around to see a small pack of people running after us.

"*¡Deja de robar las ropas!*" one yelled. The small crowd seemed to be gaining on us.

"Wonder what happened to them?" I asked Chris.

"You come back here with our clothes, you idiot," another screamed. One short pudgy man with black hair, a moustache, and white scrubs jumped and body tackled Chris onto the pavement. He and two others started yanking at the clothes Chris was helplessly clutching in his arms. Instinctively, I ran, not knowing what the hell was happening or what to do about it. Two other women, one black and wearing what appeared to be a chef's outfit and one Hispanic wearing black scrubs and a hairnet screamed words at me that I only hear when I make Reima really mad.

They caught up to me when I got to the door of my truck. "*Tu stupido gringo,*" said one, slapping me on the head while the other one started kicking me in the shins.

"Owwwwww. What is it?" I yelled.

"You stole our clothes, you bastard," the other lady screamed.

"These aren't your clothes. Somebody from our group donated them to charity. I found them on the table," I offered, still confused.

"The hell they ain't our clothes," she said. "We change every day when we come in to work and put our clothes on the back of that table. You stole 'em."

The Hispanic woman kept slapping me on the head and yelling words like "burro," "idiota," and "tonto." None of them were good.

"Okay, okay, I'm sorry; I didn't know," I said, handing their clothes to them. The Hispanic woman grabbed a shirt angrily into her fist and then shook it at me. The black woman kicked me one more time in the shin and then said, "Let that teach you, you piece of shit."

Chris staggered over to me as the small crowd walked away in a huff, expletives flying in English, Spanish, and some language I didn't recognize. Chris's cheek and nose were bleeding. "I guess those clothes weren't part of the donation," he said, wiping his nose with the back of his sleeve.

I shrugged. "You okay?" I asked, feeling even worse knowing I was the reason he got roughed up.

"I'll be fine. Just need a few Band-Aids. But boy, were they pissed!"

"Yeah," I said softly, defeated.

"You coming back in?" Chris asked.

"No, I think I've done enough damage. I'll just go home. Look, man, I'm sorry I dragged you into this, but I really thought they were donations."

"Don't worry about it," Chris said. "I mean, I'm a little pissed, but it was an honest mistake."

He walked away, and I waved at him as I got into the driver's side of my truck. I looked at the parking lot ahead of me. A couple of ripped shirts lay on the pavement, apparent casualties of Chris's battle. Then, out of the corner of my eye, I saw it: that damned box still on the passenger's seat. I'd forgotten about it. *I'll show them*, I thought. *I'll just leave it here in the parking lot and make someone else clean it up.* My rage grew, and the ideas started flooding me. *Better yet, I'll take it to the dumpster behind the shopping center and throw it in.* All the ridicule I'd just endured in the bar, the years of disappointment watching our stupid pigeon mascot act like an idiot, every vile thing that Alex had either said or directed my way, and our terrible team that we were all ashamed of—it was all wrapped up in that box. That damned box. *I'll show them.*

I put my foot on the brake and shifted the truck into gear. But before I took my foot off the brake, something dawned on me. I still didn't know for sure what was in the box. If it was something nice, like a lighter version of the license plate covers, maybe Reima and I could give them as Christmas presents. We almost never gave presents, but this would cost us nothing. It would be courtesy of the Pigeons.

I took one of my jagged keys and ran it along the crease in the box where the brown tape sealed it. I ripped open the flaps, and there, sitting in the box, were dozens of rolled-up gray T-shirts. Picking one up, I unfolded it and held it up like it was hanging on a clothesline. It was cheap material, but the shirt didn't look too bad. It had a nice emblem and the words "South Central Missouri." And, of course, over the heart was an image of a stupid pigeon. That was when I had my second brilliant idea of the night. I might not get my form signed by Alex, but at least the less fortunate would get some clothes. I wadded up the T-shirt, slung it back into the box, and took my foot off the brake. They were going in a dumpster all right, but not the one I'd originally planned.

A couple of weeks later, Reima and I decided to go to DC for dinner. We passed by the national mall in front of the Washington Monument, and we saw a rally. There were small, dirty blue tents set up all around the mall, shirtless young white guys in dreadlocks were handing out pamphlets, and it looked like the people at the rally intended to live there for a while, just like during the Occupy DC phase that happened on McPherson Square a few years ago. I glanced at their signs, trying not to make eye contact. "Homes,

Not Loans," "Gimme Shelter," "Tax the Rich," and various Bible verses about taking care of the poor were printed in red and black letters on poster boards leaning against the tents. Something else caught my gaze, but I rubbed my eyes and walked on quickly.

We kept walking, and a few minutes later, Reima said, "There sure were a lot of people from your school there. It doesn't look good that so many alumni from your university are homeless."

I pretended I didn't hear. "Feel like Italian?"

8

My Rod and My Staff Do Not Comfort Me

Everyone was gathered in the conference room when I walked in. Well, everyone but *her*. However, I got an email that she was on her way. To my surprise, NuPol was not sitting at the head of the table; he was in the spot where I usually sat. I am not sure if that was a sign of respect—most likely not—or he'd just decided to wait at least one meeting before he started messing with me. I plunged in.

"Hi, everyone. I'm glad you could join me today."

Mini forced out an exhale and shook her head. I pretended not to notice.

"As you know from the meeting with Less," I said, "I'm going to be the acting supervisor of the group for a few weeks while he is in training." "A few weeks" sounded much better to me than "a few months." Mini exhaled even louder. I don't know where all her air comes from, but she does have a lot of capacity for it.

"But, uh, we can all get through this together," I said, forcing a laugh. Only Buzz responded, giving his classic forced laugh that sounded like a car with a rundown battery trying to start. That was worse than no one laughing at all.

I cleared my throat. "I need to go to my first meeting with Less's boss tomorrow, so I guess I need to get an update on what everyone is doing."

"Hah, running with the big dogs," NuPol said with a smirk. Buzz laughed for real.

I smiled. "Well, not like I have much of a choice." I was hoping that playing the victim would get me some sympathy and cooperation.

I looked around the room to pick who would start with updates. I knew not to begin with Buzz, because it always takes him so long to tell people how busy he is.

"Let's start with you, Mini. What have you been working on?"

My victim play was for naught. "I don't think I'm comfortable talking about anything until *she* gets here."

I cleared my throat again. "But, Mini, I am only asking you what you're working on."

"I wonder what she'd say about you having a staff meeting when she's not here."

"Mini, I got an email from her," I said. "She's on the way. Now tell me what you're doing."

"You don't have all your staff here."

This time I exhaled.

"Okay, NuPol, what is going on with you?" I'm pretty sure I generally know what is going on with him, but between Mini not telling me anything and knowing that Buzz would tell me everything, I decided I needed a warm-up.

NuPol leaned forward in his chair. Apparently, he had been waiting.

"I've entered about three complaints to the Office of General Counsel. They're supposed to make a decision on one complaint this week, the Gas Policy, which means we are probably about a month away from a final resolution."

I didn't know about his two other complaints, but unfortunately, I knew all too well about the Gas Policy. This can definitely be considered a very low-brow discussion, so I'll do a favor for the efficiency guru and anyone else who may have the misfortune to find this journal and flag the next section so you can skip it.

*****BEGINNING OF TOILET PROTOCOL DISCUSSION*****

About two months ago, NuPol stepped into my cube to update me on his latest project. He had just gone to the bathroom and had been inspired to push for a new organizational policy. It seems the Deputy Secretary was at the urinal next to NuPol, and, as sometimes happens when someone is, how can I say, doing number one, a warning shot for, how can I say, number two comes along. The Deputy Secretary, or DepSec, apparently gave this olfactory warning shot, shook himself to purge excess urine, zipped up, and smacked the handle to flush. He didn't even acknowledge NuPol as he scooted over to the sink and turned on the water.

Well, NuPol was both astonished and motivated to develop a policy on when the warning shot can (or more importantly, when it cannot) be fired by someone in the bathroom. This policy would exempt those in the women's restroom, who generally sit when they pee, which would make it hard to distinguish a simple warning shot from part of something more. But NuPol was adamant that even women should not fire warning shots when they were out of the stall and in the common area of the restroom. He initially thought about excluding toilet stalls altogether; however, he was concerned that once the new policy comes out (which he calls his Gas Policy for obvious reasons), men would try to get around it by going into the toilet stalls to do number one and letting their warning shots fly. Therefore, the Gas Policy only applies to those who do number one while standing, regardless of where they do it. I know this bathroom configuration sounds old-fashioned, but we are in an old building and, at this point, still have separate men's and women's restrooms. And I have been told by NuPol (not that I would know firsthand) that there are no urinals in the women's bathroom.

Anyway, Less dispensed with his usual role of running interference in NuPol's latest projects, which never ends well for Less, and asked NuPol to work directly with the Office of General Counsel, or OGC. NuPol tackled this assignment with gusto. I saw him getting in early, working on drafts and redrafts of the Gas Policy, and simulating various scenarios—in *my* cube, no less—regarding the gray areas, such as if someone wasn't really sitting or standing but rather hovering over the toilet (or I guess urinal) as they did number one. That was the part of NuPol's process that I enjoyed the least.

It seemed that, much to the surprise of everyone (most of all Less), NuPol seemed to be getting some traction on the Gas Policy. Multiple attorneys were commenting on the policy and working with NuPol to get it finalized and signed. It seemed they (well, at least some of them) were convinced by his Policy Purpose statement that great anxiety was felt throughout the staff because there was no official language on when and under what conditions warning shots could be fired in the restroom.

NuPol was so excited to see the proposal's progress that he even started making compromises to increase the chances that the Gas Policy would become the rule for the agency. I think even he would admit that most of his actions are just to spin up management, and he never really expects most of his proposals to result in actual policy changes. But this one was different. It was like he actually had a purpose. NuPol started saying things like "legacy," words that he never used and ones I knew he didn't take lightly. One of his major concessions, which let me know that he was serious, was to allow exemptions based on a person's level in the organization. In other words, anyone at the Assistant Secretary level and above would be exempted from the policy and could fire warning shots anywhere and anytime. Also, political appointees would be exempt, and the policy would only apply to career civil servants. The attorneys working with NuPol convinced him that upper management would never sign such a policy if it limited their options for firing warning shots, so NuPol conceded. He told me that once the Gas Policy was in place, he would work on addenda that could be rolled out over time to plug those holes, so to speak. Apparently, NuPol was now in the final throes of determining the penalties for violations. I hope it is evident why I did not want to get into this level of detail at the staff meeting. Speaking of which . . .

*****END OF TOILET PROTOCOL DISCUSSION*****

There is probably nothing I cared about less—and wanted to avoid more—than a discussion of NuPol's policy efforts, but

I decided to at least give them some legitimacy and ask about next steps.

"Okay, NuPol, I think I'm up to speed on those, especially the Gas Policy," I replied, sparing myself and the staff from the painful specifics.

"I doubt it will come up at my meeting," I continued, "but just in case, are there any near-term actions that we need to take on our end?" I caught myself and braced for the jokes NuPol could make about my careless phrase "on our end." Fortunately, he let it pass, so to speak.

NuPol looked to the side and started nodding slowly as his sinister smile developed. "I was thinking about doing a demonstration video of the various scenarios. Should I start on that?"

I could only imagine the kind of video NuPol would make to support his Gas Policy proposal and could never imagine being able to view it in a room with attorneys.

"I'll have to check the budget and get back to you," I replied, employing the tactic Less used repeatedly to shut down any effort he did not want to progress.

The corners of NuPol's mouth stretched back to a straight line as his smile left and his nodding stopped.

I cleared my throat, knowing I had disappointed my friend and realizing it was the first of many times that was likely to happen while I was in this position.

I shifted my body and turned my gaze toward Buzz. I could feel myself breathe in deeply without thinking, like I was getting ready to put my head under water for a long time, and that's when we heard it: There was a bump outside that sounded like someone had run into a cubicle wall and knocked it down. This was followed by some commotion, with one voice dominating while others ceased and seemed to scatter. Then it appeared in the doorway. *She* appeared in the doorway. Mini smiled, and I thought she was going to start clapping. There she was in all her glorious self: Negativa Diva.

I cannot adequately describe the way a room changes at the appearance of Negativa Diva. It starts transforming at the very inkling that she may be arriving soon. A sense of gloom and foreboding can be felt, like fog coming out of sprinkler heads. Blurry, melting faces could be seen around the table, except for Mini's.

"Apparently, you started without me" were the first words that bellowed from the crevice in her permanently scowled face. She pushed up her 1960s-style cat-eye glasses, which seemed to be ill fitting and always fell down her nose. She was wearing her classic brown polyester pants from a bygone era and a stained white top that made her look like a life-size bowling pin.

I opened my mouth to speak, but Mini beat me to the punch. "I told him not to, but he wouldn't listen. I told him, and I didn't give an update. I would never do that without you here."

Negativa Diva slowly wobbled over to her seat, the seat that no one, not even NuPol, dared inhabit, even in her absence. It was like watching Jabba the Hutt take his throne.

"I want to know why Less chose you to act for him."

I felt my leg start to shake, and my face felt like it was on fire. My mouth went dry immediately. Hearing her voice in other meetings always made me nervous, but since her onslaughts were generally directed at Less, I never felt this sense of panic.

"Well, Negativa Diva, I am not sure. He needed someone to fill in, and he asked me," I said, voice quivering, both legs shaking now.

"I didn't see any paperwork, and I'm not sure you have the legitimacy to even hold this staff meeting," she said, eyes narrowed to a squint like focused lasers.

I had no other choice but to address this now. Negativa Diva never forgot, never gave up, and never stopped if she thought she had something on somebody else. This would go on forever, and I would not be able to have any staff meetings if I didn't push back.

I narrowed my gaze to try to match hers, though I felt that it probably looked like a forced, inferior version of the one from the master.

"Look, this decision wasn't yours, and it wasn't mine. Less made it and didn't need anyone's permission to do so. This is the situation, and we all need to live with it and do the best we can for the next few weeks."

She folded her arms and looked straight ahead and up, as if none of this were really happening. I decided to move on to Buzz so he could start reciting the numerous projects that all of us involuntarily heard about every day.

"Are you sure you want me to start?" Buzz asked. "This could take a while."

I reluctantly nodded.

As he started his classic "best of" showcase of anything he'd ever worked on in his life, my mind started to wander. First, I started wondering about the meeting tomorrow, but after bouncing around to different things, I finally settled on thinking about dinner, so my dinner ponderings were interspersed with Buzz's summary of his tasks and accomplishments.

"And they wanted the interpretation about that order back to the bureau by Friday, which I said was impossible because—" *I wonder if I should just get off the bus at Shirlington and try to go to that place that has the extended happy hour. I think sometimes they have free chips and a spinach dip.* "I told him we were starting a precedent with the new software, and some of the data on real property may not transfer over smoothly, and someone will need to QA it. The AI program made a lot of mistakes. I could develop a checklist—" *I like their spinach dip. I wonder who first came up with that spinach Maria dip. You can eat it as a side dish but also use it as a dip. Maybe it's Italian? If it had red sauce, I'd be sure it was Italian. I wish I could sneak a look at my phone and find out.* "The page numbers had to be in the upper right. She pushed back on that, but I explained . . ."

At this point, my attention was so scattered that I was only hearing two or three words at a time, and my eyelids started to droop. But I knew that Buzz would be offended if I fell asleep during his important update, so I made an effort to add in a few "hmmms" and "uh-huhs" and "interestings," all the while injecting strategically placed nods to appear to be reflecting. The conversation had devolved into Buzz's summary, *my thoughts*, and my occasional "hmmms" and "uh-huhs."

Buzz droned on: "Times New Roman font, I told him—" *I kind of like the salsa at that new taco truck out back in the Village, too. At our usual place, it seems like it's just a few tomatoes and oniony water, but this place makes it thicker.* "Fidelity to the data source is important, and—" *I wonder how the cheese place next door is. That might be a classy quest; go there and pretend to be interested in some cheese. We've been meaning to try to up our game. If I learned more about cheese, we could go to France one day, and I could just point to what I like and order. That yellow cheese, s'il vous plaît, which is all the French I know.* "And the algorithm needs to match the desired output—" *Is bocce ball considered classy? It sounds classy; it's spelled classy, and I learned about it from that dentist friend we used to hang out with when we first moved here. Dentists must know classy stuff. Hmmmm, maybe I could learn to play bocce ball.* "Oh, I almost forgot the most important thing. Fred came to me and asked—" *Wonder how dentists feel about spinach Maria dip. I mean, it has spinach, so it must be good for you. I bet they like it. But it also gets in people's teeth. Wonder if anyone goes to the dentist with spinach still in their teeth. I always brush before going to the dentist. I figure I'll at least get a passing grade if there is nothing visible on my teeth and—*

I looked up and was dramatically aware of the complete silence. Buzz had stopped talking, my thoughts had stopped, and my forced nodding had stopped. The staff meeting seemed to be frozen in time.

"Well?" Buzz asked me. "Which one should we choose?"

Oh, no. The curse of all curses in a staff meeting. Buzz wanted a decision, but I had no idea what he had been talking about. I didn't dare risk a "Could you repeat that?" because for Buzz, that often meant going back a half hour or so to the middle of his summary and starting there, so I decided to take the management way out.

"It's an interesting choice. Let me look into it and get back to you." I noticed by everyone's surprised faces that Buzz had probably asked something either obvious or stupid, but I thought the best course of action was to end the meeting on that note, looking thoughtful and contemplative, even if the decision was obvious or stupid, or both.

"Hey, we didn't give you an update," Mini said, flicking her thumb back and forth between herself and Negativa Diva. I knew this would devolve into a conversation about my illegitimacy in this new role, and there was no way I was opening that can of worms.

"Sorry, I have to get ready for another meeting," I said, telling my first lie as Acting Director. I was sure there would be many others. "Just send me an email letting me know what you have been working on." I folded my binder and heard Negativa Diva say something about fairness and equal time as I walked out the door. When I got back to my cubicle, I looked at my notes from the meeting. There were only two words: spinach Maria. I opened my browser for a history lesson.

After learning about spinach Maria, I put a "Do Not Disturb" sign on my cube. A minute later, I was surprised to see Less standing in front of me.

"I thought you were gone," I offered, hoping for a moment that he had changed his mind and I would not have to endure my temporary promotion.

"I was meeting with my boss. I just stopped to say goodbye and give you something."

Less's usual furrowed brow and look of constant constipation seemed to have already given way to normalcy, like he was going on a vacation. I walked around my desk to shake his hand and asked him, just above a whisper, "Got any advice for me?"

He looked around like we were being monitored and whispered, "Always have papers in your hand, walk fast, and look worried. Fewer people bother you." He turned to walk away but then said in a regular volume, "Oh, one more thing." He held something up in his curled fist at eye level like he was going to drop it. I dutifully held my open hand about a foot below. He opened his hand and dropped into mine a single key on a chain with a small Muppet character of Beaker. "Yours now," he said and left. I stared at Beaker for a moment and then became ecstatic. Now I saw the one advantage to being the boss. I wouldn't have to sit in this open cubicle, pretend to work, and hope to be left alone. I could now go into Less's office, close the door, pretend to work, and hope to be left alone.

A vast improvement.

9

Mini and Negativa Diva's Relationship Explained

For years, I could never really understand the relationship between Mini and Negativa Diva. When Mini first came to our group, she was social and likeable. Buzz, NuPol, and I all thought she was a great addition. She seemed interested, and even helpful, but not disruptive. However, once she got into Negativa Diva's orbit, we noticed a change as she began circling around her mother star. It was like someone had flipped a switch, and all of a sudden, she became completely subservient to Negativa Diva. Mini would disrupt meetings to express outrage at any small announcement, like they were going to paint the bathrooms the following Tuesday, so for one day only, we needed to use the bathrooms on another floor.

One time, Less sent a message saying that we should all consider contributing to the Combined Federal Campaign, the government's charity fund. He made it clear in the message that this was not mandatory, that we should all "search our own hearts" and give what we thought was appropriate. Apparently, Mini meant to forward the message to Negativa Diva, but instead, she mistakenly replied to all.

Her reply said, "I can't believe they are forcing us to do this. We need to bring him down. Tell me what you want me to do." At that point, it was clear. We'd all suspected that Mini had become Negativa Diva's lackey, but until she forwarded that email, we'd only suspected. After that, we had proof. But rather than being ashamed of the email, Mini seemed emboldened in her subservience. She didn't try to hide that she was making comments to win favor with Negativa Diva, and it seemed she would rather have direct conflict with everyone else in the department than even think an unkind thing of Negativa Diva. She would even rather clash with Less, who did her performance appraisal and recommended her raises.

Her behavior seemed bizarre to me until NuPol explained his theory, which he'd learned in a management class he'd taken. Of course, NuPol hasn't attended as many classes as Buzz, who holds the record. I don't think the classes are necessarily meant to help NuPol but to keep him occupied at least for that week. Buzz goes to training so we don't have to listen to him talk about how busy he is, and NuPol goes to give Less some relief. I guess that's really what training is for. Anyway, sometimes when NuPol comes back, he has new ideas for ways to illuminate management's transgressions, but apparently, that is a risk Less is willing to take to have some short-term peace in the office. It's not lost on me that every-one seems to be benefitting from training in some way, except for the poor idiot who has to herd the cats while Less goes to his. I'm beginning to think Reima is right. We are cursed to always get the short end of the stick.

Anyway, at that session NuPol attended, they discussed orga-nizational dynamics and personalities. One of the characteristics is the person in the office who is always stirring the pot—always trying to push everyone's buttons. To his credit, NuPol rec-ognized that he is the pot stirrer/button pusher in our office. While he was explaining it to me, I sensed pride in his voice that his position had been recognized and named but also disap-pointment that people like him occurred so often, especially in the government, that they had been categorized. NuPol really thought he had invented the archetype.

Another role is the happy go-along-to-get-along person, which NuPol pegged to be me. I would not have described myself like that, because even though I behave that way, I am not happy about it. But now that I think about it, it is as good a descrip-tion as any. Of course, there is also the suck-up, always using the corporate-speak words like "leverage," "critical skills," "vector check," etc., and that person is obviously Buzz. But then there is another strange dynamic that can develop that explains the inter-actions between Negativa Diva and Mini. It's called the Drama Triangle. NuPol let me read his slides to decipher that one.

The Drama Triangle is made up of three parts, hence the name. Picture a triangle. At one point, put "Oppressor." At another, put "Victim." And at the third point, put "Rescuer." Now what hap-pens in the Drama Triangle is that someone, who is acting in the role of the Rescuer, will pounce on a Victim and propose to save them. However, to make it work, they need an Oppressor. So the

Rescuer will identify the Oppressor and convince the Victim that they, and only they, can save the Victim. The Oppressor is usually someone in power and might not have anything to do with the Victim. The Rescuer simply needs to be able to *convince* the Victim that the Oppressor is the enemy.

Experienced Rescuers intuitively know how to find and exploit a Victim's weaknesses. They know how to spot people ripe for manipulation. The other dynamic that develops is that the Rescuer, given this power over the Victim, almost always becomes an Oppressor, but the Victim either doesn't recognize it or is too afraid to let the *previous* Rescuer (*current* Oppressor) down. Therefore, they continue being subservient to the previous Rescuer, who is now the new Oppressor, and they unfortunately stay that way.

That sounded a bit too sinister to me, but NuPol explained that it happens all the time, even from a young age. "Have you noticed," he asked, "how bullies develop victims in grade school? The victim-and-bully scenario plays out from the time people start interacting with each other until the time they stop. Hell, you can even see this happen at the other end of life in nursing homes!"

I reflected on this for a minute. That scenario would explain the bizarre relationship between Mini and Negativa Diva. I thought at first maybe they had become lovers and Negativa Diva simply had the upper hand on Mini. But I don't think even Mini—to give her some credit—could sink to the level of being Negativa Diva's lover, so Mini must be the Victim.

Let me end this by adding context. There are two women in our group, and I admit I have spoken of them rather poorly based on the insights that NuPol gave me. Nothing said here or throughout this journal should suggest that I dislike women. I like women very much and have almost nothing but good things to say about most other women I know (though I have had occasional run-ins with Alex and HO). I have a strong mother and a strong wife and great respect for women in general. So let me put to rest any notion that this is an anti-woman journal. There are good and bad people in any and all genders, but it just so happens that the two women in my group are bad ones.

Come to think of it, NuPol, Buzz, and Less are all bad too, just in different ways. I guess the only person who doesn't have a problem in our group is me. Interesting. As I mentioned in the beginning, I am being honest about my feelings in this journal. So if the truth offends, I again encourage any poor bastard who found this to stop reading it now and burn it. I suspect you will find it only gets worse.

10

Domestic Tranquility

No matter what happens at work, I know things will be okay at home. I am a white guy from a rural part of Missouri, but I had the good fortune of meeting Reima, an exotic beauty, at an international party toward the end of our college days years ago. It was a party neither of us wanted to go to. One of Reima's friends from Ecuador convinced her to go, though she protested that it was full of loser Americans who couldn't get an American woman. One of my friends from Iran convinced me to go, though I was out with a group of buddies at a bar and had no desire to leave. This later became an inside joke: that we met at a party neither of us wanted to go to—her because she only met loser Americans at those gatherings, and me because I only met loser foreigners, but only half of that was actually true. I didn't want to go to the party because I was content at the fifty-cent beer night—that's all. But all these years later, I am so glad I went and wouldn't change that night or trade my beauty from Colombia for anything.

I hear that people are the same all over, and for the most part, that's true, though my beautiful Reima has enlightened me to some of the subtle differences in her culture and mine. Well, actually, her family has probably enlightened me more than she has. She likes to say that she is Americanized, and I believe it. She complains a lot more about the Latinas who grew up here, who are whiter than me and have no accent, than she ever complains about the white Karens who live around us and seem to get waited on faster than her at clothing stores, and who grab the last decent avocado at Wegmans just as Reima is reaching for it. I guess she expects this entitlement mentality from white Karens, but she seems to resent it when the whiter-than-me Latinas who grew up here and sound more American than I do complain about how hard they have it. "They think they've had it hard," she opines in a sexy accent that I am careful never to point out; otherwise, I am invested in an hour-long rant about how she has an accent and others don't. I have learned that sometimes it's best to keep my compliments to myself.

I think we have a great relationship, which is why I was a little surprised to see a book called *An In-Depth Method for Evaluating and Detoxifying Your Relationship* on her nightstand. I wasn't being nosy—well, not really—but when I saw the colorful red and yellow book cover with a man and a woman turned away from each other with their heads in their hands, I was kind of curious. When I saw the title, I thought maybe it was about her coworkers or the Latinas that she hangs around with, because God knows they always have drama. But then I started reading it and saw that it was about her partner—that is, me.

She was downstairs watching one of her Spanish soap operas that would be on for another half hour, so I started reading the book. There were twelve chapters, and each chapter had a series of questions at the end, called "Tox-illuminators," that were meant to illustrate how you can behave in certain ways you might not even be aware of that add toxicity to your relationship. The more I read through the questions, the happier I was that she was reading this book. I could see that most of these questions could very much not only contribute to her self-improvement but improve our relationship as well. This was very helpful, and I committed to supporting her in this endeavor as much as I could.

When she slowly opened the door and scooted to the sink with a slow shuffling sound on the rug in our bedroom to brush her teeth and do her nightly ritual, I stood and walked up behind her.

"I found this on your nightstand," I said, holding the book up to the mirror, so we were looking at each other and the book's reflection.

"Yes, I just got that. I started taking a class with the Latinas. It's kind of like a support group, and that's the book they are using. I haven't even opened it."

"I think you should. Some of the questions at the end of the chapters are very helpful," I said, trying to show just how supportive I was.

She stopped mid-brush and spit out a mouthful of toothpaste/water/saliva and responded even as a trickle of white rolled from the corner of her mouth. "I don't think *I* need to read that. I'm just going to support Azelia. She and George are having all kinds of problems."

My smile dropped, as did my arm with the book to my side. My support was going to need a boost. "Might still be good to read it. We want to have the best relationship we can. We don't want to become like some of the other Latina–gringo couples we know."

She turned around to face me with a "we need to talk" look on her face that scared me a little. Then it was replaced with a slightly confused look. "We don't have a problem, do we?" she asked, enunciating the last two words.

I needed to recover quickly. "Oh, no, not at all." Then I decided retreat was the best offense at this point. I leaned in and kissed her forehead gently. "See you in bed."

The next day, I reflected on our conversation and thought it was time to give it another go to get her to read the questions and improve herself and, in turn, us. I picked up my phone to call her and saw that she was calling me. I hit the green button to answer. "I was just going to call you," I said happily.

I said, "I think you need to read the book" just as she said, "I think you need to take the class."

"What?" I asked.

"George is trying to get a group of the gringos married to Latinas together and take this class. I thought you'd like to do it, since you like the book so much."

"Actually, I was calling to tell you I think you really need to read the book and answer the questions," I said sternly.

There was silence for a few seconds; then I decided to break it. "I'll see you at home."

"Bye," she said and hung up.

I knew that was the end of our relationship improvement journey. Not surprisingly, she never went to the class, and I avoided George's phone calls for a week until his name stopped showing up on my screen. I saw the book on top of the garbage when I was taking it out, and I knew where we stood. I kind of think we both felt empowered. We are fine, our relationship is good, and the forces that be will try to improve us over our dead bodies.

In the midst of this, Reima and I recently finished another relationship milestone: fertility treatment. Not that we really wanted kids, but it is a necessary rite of passage for a married couple to (1) have children, (2) try to have children, or (3) take care of someone else's children. Well, we had not done the first and didn't really like kids, so we couldn't do the third, so it left us with only one option.

I probably shouldn't admit this, even to a journal no one else will ever see, but I have a dark secret. I see one big advantage in having a kid: REVENGE. I really would like to have a baby of my own that is bald, with a big bobble head, that I could take out when we meet people for dinner. We could dress him or her in stupid clothes with stains all over them, sit there pretending to be oblivious as sundry materials come out of their mouth or nose, and force our dinner companions to lie by serving up such zingers as "Isn't he cute?" and "Don't you love that face?" Then, once they lie and say that my little creature is adorable as they try not to regurgitate, I would start my interrogation and trap them with some variation of, "Who do you think he/she looks like?" I look forward to the odd glances and uncomfortable squirming that will inevitably lead to an answer like "I can see both of you in him/ her." Women are unusually good liars here, for they immediately start talking about what body parts look like which parental unit. "Oh, I can see your eyes and his chin." "He has your neck." I love this one, because no newborn critters have their parent's neck; they all have the same unstable fatty mass that comes off the shelf from the land of necks for newborns.

I mostly just want to have a kid for the holidays, but not for the reason you think. I want to have the ugliest kid and take a picture of them sitting on a stained quilt with snot coming out of their nose during the height of all their drool glory, slap it on a card, and send it out for Christmas.

This will be the gift that keeps on giving. They will have to look at our droolboy/droolgirl, write me back, and tell me how beautiful this creature is (lie 1), debate about whether or not to tell me they are offended by a "Christmas" card (lie 2—they really don't give a shit; they just want to follow DC culture trends), and keep the picture because, of course, you can never throw those things away. We have hundreds of cards of ugly kids who look like a drooling Mr. Potter from *It's a Wonderful Life* in case we ever need to produce them on demand to prove we are not jealous, baby-hating nonbreeders. Apparently, the fates saw through my scheme, and droolboy/droolgirl went to another couple with purer intentions.

Failing at this, we fostered a dog. I kind of liked it, but the first time I was out of town and Reima had to take it for a walk and clean up its shit with a plastic grocery bag that, unbeknownst to her, had a hole in it, that was the end of that. No more fostering, no more pets, and no more Aces. We moved on.

11

Previous Amusing Oddity/Current Problem

The next day, I went straight to Less's, now my, office. Not only was his office of great benefit to me, but his advice was as well. I made sure I had papers with me when I got off the train. They were all blank and bunched up together, but I clutched them to my side like they were precious X-rays I had to show to a doctor. I put on my best worried look by wrinkling my forehead, but as I stared at my dull reflection in the silver metal elevator wall, I wasn't sure if even I believed it. I took a deep breath as the elevator doors opened. *Here goes*, I thought. I walked fast once I got off the elevator, straight to "my" office about twenty steps away.

It worked. Well, it kind of worked. Both Buzz and Mini were apparently waiting for me to get off the elevator, but I fended them off in quick succession. I felt like a warrior running a gauntlet. I mumbled, "Gotta get ready for a meeting." Buzz tried to walk beside me and say that he just needed a minute, but I knew if I stopped, it would mean utter defeat. In Buzz time, a minute could be hours, so I fumbled to open the door to my new office, dropping Beaker and the key. "Sorry, I have a lot to review," I mumbled, shutting the door in the middle of his sentence. It felt wonderful. I wonder if Less felt that way on the few occasions he'd done that to me or the many times he'd done that to Buzz.

I logged onto Less's computer with my password. Less had a huge monitor in the middle of the desk, I assume so he would not have to look at anybody who entered. It was a powerful shield to hide behind and intimidate others. I opened my weekly calendar, which was now populated with Less's—*my*—meetings. They looked like a patchwork of squares on a quilt. *Is this all Less does—go to meetings? When does he work? Oh, now I get it. Counseling NuPol is probably the only work he actually does.*

The next meeting was coming up at 10:00 a.m., and when I saw the topic, it felt like it was flashing in huge font. It was Less's "Meeting with Peers." This is the dreaded meeting he tells us about. I don't know if he fears it or just wants us to fear it. Less paints the picture that it's as dysfunctional as our staff meetings, hard as that is to believe. I needed some advice on how to handle this, and then I remembered that NuPol went to it once. I think it had been a strategy by Less to try to shake NuPol up and make him behave for fear he may have to attend another one. I knew it would take more than that to intimidate NuPol, but sadly, Less didn't. NuPol seems to be Less's white whale, to use a literary analogy from grade school—and a classic book of the day from my literary calendar. (Note to self, I need to get my word-of-the-day and literary calendars from my cube and bring them in here.)

NuPol hadn't told me much about the content of the meeting but had given me a rundown of the Office Directors, including who sat where and what he thought that meant. I knew I needed to consult with NuPol ASAP on how to get through it. On cue, Buzz simultaneously knocked and opened my door. "You got a minute for that update now?" he asked.

I wormed my head out from behind my big screen and said, "I really don't, but could you send NuPol in?"

"NuPol hasn't come into the office yet," he said, sounding disappointed that he wasn't going to get face time with me. I can't imagine anybody wanting that or thinking it was important.

"Okay," I said when he didn't move. "We'll talk after my meeting this morning." That seemed to suit him because he left, and I got back up and shut the door.

I strategically waited until about 9:50 a.m. to open the door and walk out of my office. That would barely give me time to make the meeting so I could legitimately say I was in a hurry. As soon as I opened the door, my worst fear materialized. Negativa Diva was standing right in front of me with her arms crossed.

"NuPol is AWOL. You need to address this," came her gravelly voice out of the Jabba crevice. I admit it was quite jarring. Blowing off Buzz was one thing, but Negativa Diva was another matter. She would do anything, and I mean *anything*, to cause problems. One time after the Secretary committed to transparency, she asked for a meeting to discuss an important issue. The issue, we later learned, was that she preferred Post-it Notes with lines, and Less had ordered regular ones with no lines. The Secretary was overseas during that time, so the Deputy Secretary had to take the meeting. When the Deputy Secretary sized up how persistent Negativa Diva was, he agreed to take care of the matter. Long story short, Negativa got her lines, and Less got scolded for letting someone from his staff bother the DepSec with something so stupid. Less offered to let Negativa order the office supplies after that, but she refused. So he delegated that task to Buzz, which is one of the pressing issues in his portfolio that he has to discuss at length daily.

I knew what worked with others wouldn't work with Negativa, but I really had no choice but to play the late card. "I'll deal with that after my meeting." That meeting was my crutch to avoid everything.

But never underestimate Negativa Diva. She strategically throws out phrases that will make her look like she cares and you don't. "You have an employee who's AWOL, and you don't care? That should be your main concern."

I knew that Negativa didn't care at all about NuPol. In fact, he was the closest thing to a rival that she had in the office and the only one who brought any sense of balance. We had an office pool going a few months ago on who could get rid of Less first, and how. My money was on NuPol, who would literally drive him crazy, and he would come into the office one day, gangster style, looking for revenge, though most money was on Negativa. The money is still there, somewhere, and I wonder if there's already a pool growing for me and my tenuous tenure.

I had to say something. In the spirit of "I care but can't deal with it now," I conjured up the eight-year-old me from a school play all those years ago when I forgot my lines and had to improvise. I was able to fake my way through it, and the audience was none the wiser. To this day, that is still one of the highlights of my life. So I stepped in close to Negativa and said, "Of course I care, more than anyone. He is not only a coworker but a friend. My heart is breaking. I must go to this meeting with Less's peers now, but I promise you one thing: At that meeting, I'll make sure we have and use every resource available to find NuPol and bring him here safely." I was kind of proud of that last-minute ad lib part. But I underestimated Negativa Diva's ability to take anything and parse it into a complaint.

"So you're friends. That means you will favor him over the rest of us," she said, not missing a beat.

I stood still for a moment and then clutched my papers more tightly, furrowed my brow, and sprinted toward the elevator as I mumbled, "No time to lose." I knew I had not won the battle, only escaped it. But I would live to fight another battle, which I knew would probably be right after the meeting.

12

Meeting with Less's Peers and a Lesson in Acronopoly

I had an ominous feeling walking into the large conference room. The focal point was a fireplace with flags beside it, both the US flag and our agency flag, anchored in a floor stand and forming a V shape. A long rectangular table, I'd guess five feet wide and fifteen feet long with designs on the sides, sat in the middle of the room. Blue curtains with gold tassels framed the two large windows that looked out over the National Mall. Five chairs sat on each side of the table with a seat at the head for Less's supervisor, a.k.a. More of Less.

Everyone was already in the room and seated, a scene I'd hoped to avoid until Negativa Diva derailed my plans. I'd wanted to get there right on time and pray that nobody noticed me until the meeting was over. I glanced up at the huge clock over the fireplace. I learned from the guys in the infrastructure group that these old clocks are notoriously wrong, generally because they are too hard to set or need parts that aren't around anymore. But this one read 9:58, which I prayed was correct because it meant I wasn't late. Still, everyone was glaring at me as if they expected an apology.

I cleared my throat. "I'm Ace. I'm here from Less's group." Then I thought a little white lie wouldn't hurt, especially since this was my first time. "This meeting just popped up on my calendar. I thought it started at ten."

All the heads around the table turned from me to Less's boss, More of Less, who was sitting at the head. They seemed to be looking for permission to let me stay. I pictured a flock of birds that fly in a V formation, where one bird is at the front and the others follow that lead.

"We do start at ten," More of Less said. "Have a seat." He waved his hand toward the table. The only seat open was near the end, farthest away from More of Less. I was glad for two things: It was far away from him, and it was facing the window. Hopefully, I would not be called on and could look out the window and daydream.

I tried to quietly sneak to my seat, but my shoe got tangled in a wrinkle in the wine-colored rug, and I stumbled a bit, only catching myself by grabbing the chair two seats up from mine. "Watch the rug," came the reflexive bark of the man sitting there.

My first thought was to say, "Why do you have a wrinkle in the rug? More like watch the wrinkles, fat ass." But the other side of my brain scampered down to my mouth before that came out, and I only mumbled, "Sorry," just above a whisper. I slinked into the chair at the end, realizing that what should have been the easiest part of the meeting for me, showing up and sitting down, had already devolved into an embarrassing spectacle.

More of Less looked at the large clock and said, "Well, it's ten o'clock. Let's get started. First, an update on the initiative to find an otherly abled person. You may recall that the judge's injunction indicates that we have to continue to pursue initiatives like this, at least in the short term. We have found a person who has a bad stutter, and we are checking with OGC to see if they have to be completely unable to speak before we can count them." Heads nodded, but I wondered if, secretly, eyes were rolling as well, like they had when this came up in our last staff meeting. Either way, I was glad they found someone, as I didn't relish having that conversation again with my staff.

I looked around the room and noticed the lineup was no accident. I recognized people from the annual Christmas party, which they started calling a "holiday" party a few years ago. It is one of the few times they allow the riffraff like me to mingle with the higher-ups, although the higher-ups really only mingle with themselves and ignore anyone else who happens to worm their way into the sacred space. Buzz always tries to mingle and gets ignored. Watching that happen is the best part for NuPol and me; it's like our present.

People were seated based on their importance to the organization, at least from the viewpoint of More of Less. The Directors of PR and Events sat on opposite sides of the table. I now remembered that NuPol had mentioned to me that he thought they were placed that way to encourage them to fight, since there was some overlap in their functions.

The only other woman in the room was the Director of Appreciation (formerly known as the Director of Diversity until the

Bureau for Logistics Optimization and General Efficiency, a.k.a. BLOGE, came along), who was now sitting at the end of the table directly across from me. So because of BLOGE, she was now DOA. Even I saw the irony in that. I knew her role was in trouble when the BLOGE guys came into the building, but some judge in Puerto Rico said they had to keep her. I guess the compromise was to change her function from diversity to appreciation. But I kind of wonder, appreciation for what? Certainly not diversity. I'm glad I don't have her job.

The lines between positions and functions have always been a bit blurred in the government, but since BLOGE started "helping" us, the blurry lines have become like fuzzy shadows in an obscure corner of a murky forest at night. (Wow, I really like that image. I need to write that down.) Anyway, I forgot what she looked like at the party last year and probably wouldn't have recognized her anyway, but I knew her pronouns because we got a series of emails before the administration changed about her bravery when her pronouns changed. There was also a reception that everyone was invited to, but everyone understood the reception was only for the higher-ups. We knew it was only for the higher-ups because the email said at the bottom in bold letters, "Employees must get permission from their supervisor to attend." NuPol tried that once, but Less just kept putting him off by saying that he had to talk to his boss, who apparently never replied to such a bold request as to let an underling attend a party that everyone was invited to. NuPol snuck into one a couple of years ago anyway but came back looking flustered. He never told me what happened, which was unusual, but if even NuPol couldn't invade that revered space, there was no way that I could.

Back to the conference table arrangements, which looked like this:

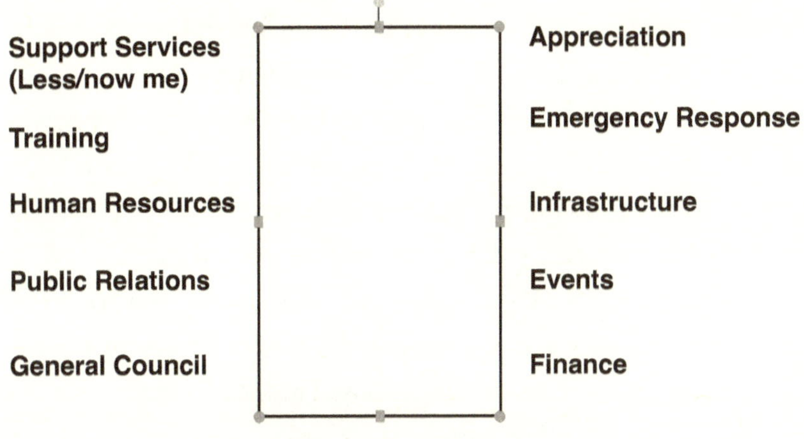

PR and Events being close to More of Less made sense to me, because they were the ones who interfaced with the public, and Events sometimes brought important people into the building. A couple of years ago, we had a Combined Federal Campaign charity event that we do once a year (which is another time that the management cares about the riffraff and tells us to donate to the campaign so they can look good). Some movie stars that nobody ever heard of were there, along with someone who got a bronze medal in the Special Olympics several years ago. All I remember is that the directors of these two departments kept getting their pictures taken with the invited dignitaries, but when the rest of us lined up to do so, they said the dignitaries had other obligations and the event was ending, so we had to go back to our offices.

The other slots around the conference table went to HR and Infrastructure (keep the people happy and the lights on, but they are really of middle-tier importance), Training (because we like to say our people are our greatest asset), and Emergency Response (which seems to have an enormous budget for conducting only one exercise a year, when we all have to just click a button to respond that we are at our desks). I was surprised that the OODIE Director who Less mentioned was not there and assumed that maybe she reported to the Director of Appreciation but later learned she reports to some low-level supervisor. Apparently, we celebrate the otherly abled but really don't appreciate them. My group is Support Services, which is a bit undefined and seems to boil down to tasks that no other group wants to do, like maintaining policies and creating memos for new positions. These tasks sound like HR functions, but since HR apparently thinks these responsibilities are beneath them, they fall to us. Nothing is beneath us.

General Counsel and Finance being closest to More of Less made sense because these were obviously the two things that mattered most to the organization: keeping the money and legal issues straight. NuPol always says the worst thing you can do to a manager in the federal government is to embarrass them. They can waste money and fail at every program they initiate, but they won't be concerned unless there is a scandal involving them that is in *The Washington Post.*

BLOGE has tried to embarrass as many federal managers as possible but made a lot of mistakes early on, so I guess BLOGE really hasn't added much value, because we feds were doing just fine embarrassing ourselves before they came along. The real value that BLOGE has brought seems to be that they have proven the only thing worse than having a flawed government is trying to fix it.

After the good news about the stutterer, More of Less opened with some platitude about how it was good to see everyone after the last week. He said to remind all our staff about how much management appreciates the hard work they are doing. We all went around the table and voiced our preferred pronouns, something we have to keep doing after a judge's injunction (though Less sometimes forgets); then he opened up the meeting, and everyone started complaining about their staff. They did it in a very, how do I say, polite way, which made the managers look like they were taking the blame while they threw their staff under the bus. They would say things like, "I need to do a better job motivating my people to meet deadlines," or "I assumed that was taken care of, but I think I trust people too much, which is my greatest fault."

I pretended to take notes, looking down and trying not to make eye contact like most people do when they are walking by panhandlers, but I really didn't hear anything worth noting. A part of me thought I might learn something, like what all these departments really did, but my naïve assumption was put to rest almost immediately. In the current environment, these offices seemed as bad as ours. I guess one thing all the efforts at efficiency have done is to bring more interoffice conflict, which makes me wonder if that was one of the goals. The managers' complaints about their staff became repetitive, and I started zoning out, thinking about places for lunch. I wanted to get out of the building. Maybe I would walk to Georgetown. It was a bit of a hike, but—

"Ace, what are your thoughts?"

Oh, no, my happy ponderings about lunch were interrupted by an unfair expectation to contribute.

I stopped doodling and looked up, attempting not to look terrified as all eyes were on me. I tried to remember the last words that were said, but all I could think about was the Ethiopian restaurant in Georgetown and wondering if it was open for lunch. Then I felt a spark. The general theme of the conversation was that the staff sucks, but the Director was pretending to take the blame because they let the staff suck.

I cleared my throat. "Yes," I said, and nodded. "I agree with everything that has been said." I could still feel the eyes on me and saw squinting from the other side of the table, so I knew they needed more. I cleared my throat again. "You know, I was late getting here because I was trying to help one of my staff members deal with a problem they had related to distractions from others, which hindered their focus on their own work." I saw the squinting stop—a good sign—then I added, "After all, it's about the mission of the organization for the American people." I looked around; everyone was nodding. Even I didn't know what I meant, but it worked, and I didn't even have to go to Less's charm school.

Then came the time in the meeting that NuPol had told me about. He liked to call this portion Acronopoly. And it was quite the spectacle, as I would soon find out. It was like watching two wild beasts in the tundra circling each other, engaging in a fight to the death. It is hard to really capture in words, but I will try my best.

I don't know exactly what prompted the start of Acronopoly because I was still basking in my clever recovery from earlier. More of Less was saying something—and then it began. The mood in the room changed, and I'm sure if this was a movie, the windows would have flown open and a gust of air would have surged in, blowing out lit candles around the room. (Sadly, the windows were sealed shut, and there were no candles.) Apparently, there was some event being planned for the following month, and both the PR and Events Directors were involved. The discussion was about a person I didn't know, but they'd run for president years ago, and someone somewhere in Washington would recognize their name. They were writing a book and coming to our agency for a visit.

The Events beast started circling the tundra first, and then PR joined in. Their tusks and claws were words, yet they had learned to say things so syrupy sweet that they could insult you and you would thank them without realizing why. *Fascinating.* I scribbled notes furiously to memorialize this sighting. Here was the real-time scene:

Events: "Well, we can just follow past patterns, but I think we need an IPT."

PR (clearing throat): "While an IPT could potentially achieve the goal, it is more appropriate in this case to make arrangements with a CTT."

Events (smiling and then clearing throat): "Hmmm. A CTT could be used by some with some effect, but now that I reflect further, it really calls for an ALG."

PR (smiling, clearing throat, and then leaning forward): "Oh. Well, some could find an ALG to add an amount of value, but what I believe the situation calls for is more of an FTS."

Events (smiling, clearing throat, leaning forward, and putting elbows on the table): "Look, the BLUF would indicate that we may need an FTS to accomplish certain objectives that will enable the goal but would need to be supplemented with a CSC."

PR (same posture as before): "Well, for that level of effort, we need to develop the SLA for them. Do you have the bandwidth to develop an SLA?"

The Events Director maintained eye contact for a few seconds and then slowly slid back in her seat, taking her previously tee-peed arms on the table with her. She dropped her gaze to the table and didn't say a word. PR had won. Apparently, PR knew an acronym that Events didn't, and that final thrust of the tusk had carried the day. I don't know why, but I felt a sense of pride that my side of the table had won this round of Acronopoly.

More of Less sensed the defeat and the need to let the bloody Events beast go away and lick her wounds in peace. He added to the throat clearing and then mercifully said, "Sounds good. Just keep me informed. We're almost out of time anyway. Any reopeners?"

Obviously, no one was going to offer anything after this monumental battle that we had all witnessed. It would be like jumping in the boxing ring and challenging someone after the Muhammad Ali–Sonny Liston fight. We had seen the pinnacle of this wilderness warfare, and there was nothing to do now but reflect and wonder. More of Less closed by saying, "Okay, have a good lunch, and see you next week."

I was far too excited to go to lunch. The Ethiopian restaurant would be there later. First, I had to get back to my office and research what I had just witnessed. As I got off the elevator, Negativa Diva was standing with Mini, as if they had been waiting for me. Mini opened her mouth and spoke, channeling Negativa Diva's thoughts. "NuPol is still not here."

Negativa Diva glared at me.

My first instinct would normally have been to say something polite to defuse the situation. But even I, the consummate people pleaser, could not waste time at the moment making others feel like I cared. I was on a mission to find out more about this fascinating battle of Acronopoly.

"I'll handle it," I said, brushing between them with a stern, "*Excuse* me."

I heard a "Huh" from Negativa Diva, the only direct offering she had for this hallway meeting, not like a question but like a response to an insult.

I went into my office and closed the door. I had to find out what all these beautiful acronyms meant so I could use them in my own battles with the staff. A well-placed acronym could fell the mightiest of beasts, and I was definitely on a collision course with Negativa Diva. I must learn the rules of this method and secure my mastery of it. I looked at my notes and feverishly searched online and through emails to learn what each acronym meant.

The first thing I discovered was that most of the phrases I heard were not acronyms at all, but initialisms. Apparently, an acronym is a collection of letters that you can say as a word, like OSHA or LASER. But an initialism is a collection of letters that you do not say as a word and sound out each letter, like FBI or CIA (which you don't pronounce as "see ya"). But most people use the term "acronym" for both, and since nobody else will ever read this journal—certainly not anyone who knows grammar, because everyone relies on AI to write anything complicated— I'll just refer to everything here as an acronym too. Besides, Initialopoly just doesn't have the same ring to it.

This is what I was able to piece together from the earlier meeting, and what it would have sounded like if government managers could talk like normal people. In some cases, the acronyms had multiple meanings, but I think I got them right based on the context. The only one I am still working on is the last acronym, the one that struck the final blow.

Events: "Well, we can just follow past patterns, but I think we need an IPT (Integrated Project Team)."

PR (clearing throat): "While an IPT could potentially achieve the goal, it is more appropriate in this case to make arrangements with a CTT (Concentrated Tiger Team)."

Events (smiling and then clearing throat): "Hmmm. A CTT could be used by some with some effect, but now that I reflect further, it really calls for an ALG (Ad Hoc Logistics Group)."

PR (smiling, clearing throat, and then leaning forward): "Oh. Well, some could find an ALG to add an amount of value, but what I believe the situation calls for is more of an FTS (Focused Tactical Squad)."

Events (smiling, clearing throat, leaning forward, and putting elbows on the table): "Look, the BLUF (Bottom Line Up Front) would indicate that we may need an FTS to accomplish certain objectives that will enable the goal but would need to be supplemented with a CSC (Comprehensive Strategy Crew)."

PR (same posture as before): "Well, for that level of effort, we need to develop the SLA for them. Do you have the bandwidth to develop an SLA?"

It was late, around 1:15 p.m., but I decided to take that lunch break after all. My training for battle (in the form of online searches and internal emails) had worn me out, and I was in need of sustenance. I grabbed a handful of papers, opened my door, and hoofed it to the elevator, feigning a worried look. Fortunately, I did not see anyone before I got on the elevator, though I heard Mini yell, "Ace!" from behind me as I stepped on. I pushed the "Close Door" button rapidly and repeatedly as her face materialized and then disappeared through the closing slit.

As the elevator descended and floor numbers flashed and then disappeared, I couldn't help but think in acronyms. Elevator going down, EGD. When it didn't stop on the way to the first floor, I realized I was on the express elevator today, EET. I felt like a gladiator who'd found a gun hidden in his loincloth, ready to use the next time I entered the coliseum. I knew I was on my way, OMW!

13

The NuPol Problem

I sat at the table in Georgetown looking out the window at M Street. The Ethiopian restaurant was plain beige inside, like a hospital room, but the red curtains gave the place some color and character. The only other people who were still there during my late lunch were part of a group of twenty-somethings who must have decided to take off early from work because they really seemed to be enjoying the mead.

I pinched off a piece of the injera bread and used it to scoop up some yellow lentils. I have never considered myself a sophisticated person, but I really like Ethiopian food. We first tried it with another couple in our neighborhood about five years ago, and I was hooked, though I rarely eat it. In Washington, DC, liking any kind of food other than American (or basically liking anything not American) is considered sophisticated. In the rare opportunities I have to be around DC-ites who like to make fun of my accent, I always seize the opportunity to change the subject to food. About the only non-American cuisine I can talk about besides Italian, Mexican, and Chinese is Ethiopian. No one here is impressed with Italian, Mexican, or Chinese since those restaurants are everywhere, but the DC-ites seem impressed with Ethiopian.

The volume at the twenties' table seemed to increase a few decibels with every round, and I decided I needed to get back to the office anyway. I strolled back and could almost see myself smiling. I reflected on the day. I had successfully recovered and presented myself well at the meeting with Less's peers, I had evaded Mini and Negativa Diva, and I had eaten sophisticated food that I could talk about for the next few months to make me seem smart. Not bad.

Nothing would bother me today. That is, until the elevator doors opened to reveal Mini standing on one side and Negativa Diva on the other, almost like palace guards. I debated on closing the doors again and leaving for the day but realized this is part of my job now, albeit one I hate.

"Where have you been?" Mini asked, scowling. Her face and those words wiped away any joy I was feeling.

"Meetings," I said, trying to deflect as I stepped off the elevator. "There's a lot going on."

They both looked down at my torso, and for a moment, I wondered if they had X-ray glasses. "Meetings, huh? I don't see any papers," Mini said. These two have a strange telepathic relationship, and I had no doubt that Negativa Diva shared the same thought that Mini had said aloud.

Oh, crap, I thought. I'd left my notebook and papers at the restaurant. I was without my tools and felt like an acrobat without a net. Then I had a moment of inspiration and said something I'd heard Less use one time when he was talking to Buzz. "It was a meeting about sensitive issues, and I had to leave my notes in the secure area."

Mini and Negativa Diva didn't seem ready for that response, so I nodded and was able to breeze past them, but not before I heard behind me, "NuPol finally showed up."

"I'll take care of it," I muttered, only loud enough for them to know I said something but not loud enough to know what it was. Another escape, built on another lie. *How did Less handle this stuff?*

I stepped into my office and picked up the phone to call NuPol. Then I hesitated. I knew I had to confront him about his tardiness, and I needed to do it here rather than in his cubicle for the world to see. I had to prepare. A new mound of moisture gathered under my arms, and I wondered if it was because of the brisk walk back or a reaction to my upcoming confrontation with NuPol.

I first decided that I needed to look the part. I didn't have another notebook, so I decided to look in Less's desk drawers to see if I could find one. There were three drawers on the left side. The top two had an assortment of pens, a few Post-it notes (without lines), business cards that looked frayed and stained, and gift cards to local restaurants. I looked at one and realized that the restaurant had closed about five years earlier. When I tried the bottom drawer, it was locked, which piqued my curiosity, but I'd deal with that later. As for now, I would have to go to battle without my props.

I needed to work with what I had, so I looked around the office to prepare my fortress. I gathered my stapler (which was empty), a red plastic cup that held some old pens, the tape dispenser (which was empty), the small paper clip holder (which was empty), and the business cards and set them in a semicircle on my desk beside the monitor. I took the Post-it Notes and put them in the middle. Since I didn't have a notepad, they would have to do. I chose a pen, held it in my fingers, and picked up the phone.

After a few minutes, NuPol came into my office and plopped down in the guest chair. He had a don't-bother-me look on his face and cocked his head to one side, looking at the floor in front of the desk. I don't think he even noticed the fortress I had meticulously created on top of it. I thought I'd break the ice with small talk.

"How are you doing? Is everything okay?" I felt myself swallow hard. This was really our first one-on-one moment after my move from friend to boss. He rolled his eyes upward without moving his head and huffed through his nose the way some people do when they're too uninterested to muster an actual laugh.

"NuPol?" I said with a questioning tone.

He did the nose huff again and this time supplemented it with a small chest heave. This wasn't going anywhere.

I cleared my throat. "NuPol, the reason I am asking if you are okay is because a lot of people were worried when you were late."

At this, he rocked back, looked upward, and finally smiled. "Worried?" he repeated incredulously. Then, he finally looked down and made eye contact with me. It was jarring.

"They don't care about me, or you. You know that, right? They just want to make things difficult for you. If you look the other way, they'll complain to the higher-ups. That's what I'd do."

"If you know that, then why did you show up late without telling me?" I asked. "Why put me in that position?"

At that, he actually laughed, not just nose-huffed. "Wow, they got to you already. You're sounding like one of them."

I decided to drop the boss tone and use the friend tone. "NuPol, look, it's me. We're friends. I covered for you, but I want to be able to answer when people ask where you are. I don't think that's too much to ask. If you won't keep me informed because I'm the boss, then do it because I'm your friend."

He stood up and leaned over the desk, getting about a foot

from my face. I could smell his coffee breath. I swallowed hard again and dropped my pen to the floor. "As long as you are in this position, even if it is temporary, you are *not* my friend. In the future, just tell them you sent me on an assignment." He looked down at the top of the desk, and my eyes followed his. Then he looked back up. "Nice fort. Less tried that early on with me. But you need better supplies. Maybe get a laptop and put that between us. Less kept getting props that were bigger and higher until one day he put a cardboard box on his desk that was so large he couldn't even see past it for conversations like this one. I barely touched the damn thing, and it fell over onto him. It's still there in the corner if you want to try that."

I looked in the corner, said a string of "uhs," and thanked him. Then my computer chimed—my next meeting. He looked sideways at the monitor, did another nose huff, and then turned and walked out.

So that was how it was going to be: me and NuPol playing a game of chicken. I was sure he would win eventually; after all, he had practiced on Less for years. But I had to maintain my dignity. After I heard his feet shuffling away and I was sure he couldn't hear me anymore, I said bravely but softly, "And *don't* forget it." I felt daring, dejected, and disappointed, all at the same time.

14

Still Doing My Other Job: The DRIP Subcommittee

I am not sure whether it is a blessing or a curse—probably a blessing given my altercation with my old friend and apparent new enemy, NuPol—but I still have to do my other job. They refer to this as being dual-hatted. Though I am usually not looking forward to my next meeting, the chime reminder served to break the tension between me and NuPol, and to be honest, I kind of wanted to be anywhere other than my office. My meeting was in the adjacent building, where my staff could not find me.

I don't really have plum assignments, not that there are any since we became more efficient, but it really seems that I always get the pit of the plum. During our better times before I became boss, NuPol told me that I needed to stand up for myself more, but I'm not sure what his advice would be now that we're adversaries. I don't volunteer for these tasks, but I get "volun-told" for things because I am too agreeable and do not duck fast enough. At first, Less was timid, almost apologetic, when asking me to do demeaning assignments. But lately, I think he defaults to "Shit task, great for Ace."

Now that I am in his seat—so to speak—for the moment, I kind of understand why. If he gives the tasks to Buzz, he'll come back and have even more to talk about, and the little that our group gets done now will be imperiled. If NuPol gets any assignments, he will figure out a way to use them to launch a complaint against Less. If Less gives something to Mini, she will immediately charge into Negativa Diva's cubicle and then come back with a list of demands and complaints. And of course, he can never give such assignments to Negativa Diva. That would ruin his well-crafted strategy of marginalizing and isolating her so she has less exposure to anyone outside our group. So . . . these tasks fall to me.

I had been in meetings in this room before, but I really noticed my surroundings this time. Unlike the conference room of my meeting with Less's colleagues and boss, the first thing that hit me here was the stench and general depressing look. The room smelled dank. Also, in contrast to the plush room of my earlier meeting with the red padded executive chairs, windows with elegant drapes, and a big cherry table in front of a fireplace, the table and chairs in this place looked like the furniture I saw in army surplus stores as a kid in southern Missouri. There was chipped, dull lime-green paint on the wall and black growths on many of the discolored, porous beige tiles above us.

The room felt different, though the desire to one-up and shine started almost immediately after the remainder of the people walked in. I never cared to count before, but there were eleven. For some reason, I am noticing things I never did.

After our pronoun check-in, the meeting started. "Okay, who has a safety share?" bellowed Vi, the leader of our subcommittee.

We always start this meeting with safety shares. We started doing that years ago, when we got a blast email to everyone that talked about how employees were the most valuable assets to the agency and how much they cared about us. And to prove it, they wanted us to start every meeting with a safety share so we will all be reminded to be safe. That part of the email came just before they announced our salaries were frozen again for the coming year. Some people leading meetings had done away with this requirement, but the leaders of this one were sticklers for protocol.

Safety shares are the first time in the meeting that someone can shine, but participation is uneven. During some meetings, people are chomping at the bit to talk about something unsafe they did and share the lesson with the rest of us, but other times, people just sit there, unable to either recollect or own up to their own stupidity. After a few seconds, Vi jumped in and said, as she always does during these moments, "Don't everybody talk at once." She forced a laugh, and everyone forced one as well, as we always do.

Someone, or multiple ones, eventually speaks up, but every so often, they like to be begged. This is a different cast of characters, so now might be a good time for me to take a minute and introduce the main voices.

- *Vi*, as in ObVIous, who always says obvious things in meetings. Examples include, "It is more efficient when we can do more with less."

- *Claude*, like a clown. Always makes inappropriate jokes.

- *Train*, because he goes to training every year and spends the rest of the year repeating the buzzwords, like "critical skills," "hot wash," etc. Train and Buzz are kindred spirits.

- *Taliban*—Talks A Lot Indefinitely But About Nothing. Self-explanatory. Taliban and Buzz are also kindred spirits.

- *Aidon*—Ain't Doing Nothing. Used to run this group but now just drops in as an honorary member.

- *Walt*—Worst-case And Literally Terrible. To Walt, things are always bad, and they will get worse, especially if we have the misguided judgment to try to fix them.

To spend a minute on Walt, he really fills the critical role of reeling us back in, especially if we try to make progress on something before we have exhaustively done our AOA. (This is my own little contribution to Acronopoly.) AOA is the Analysis of Alternatives. He has shut down terrible initiatives, such as switching pencil suppliers, as he was adamant that the new ones might have lead paint and that everyone would become mentally impaired. When I relayed this Spartacus-like act of courage by him to NuPol, he pointed out that we wouldn't really be able to tell any difference with most people. However, I started using mechanical pencils after that (on the rare occasions that I actually write something), but now it is difficult to get the lead refills because Walt successfully got a moratorium put on all things "lead," even though the safety department declared that it was not even really lead. Walt held firm that we couldn't take any chances. So now, I usually just don't write anything down and forget it like everybody else.

I think this is the way Walt generally sees the world:

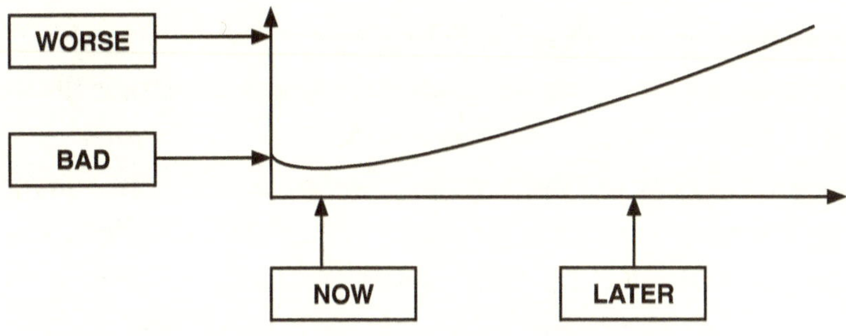

I keep my college degree working by developing graphs like this one that show how pieces of the world work. And I don't even need artificial intelligence to help me. NuPol has praised my art, especially when it illustrates the flaws of others. But anyway, back to the meeting.

Vi was an obvious choice to lead this important group. Before she led it, it was led by Aidon, which was nice because he never made us do anything as a committee. Aidon had been a supervisor before and brought those critical skills as a leader. Whenever anyone asked him why our committee didn't do much, he would simply criticize whoever was asking. The pandemic was really his heyday, because everybody expected us to meet but didn't expect us to really do anything: our sweet spot. I think the fact that he often talks about getting ready to retire means he doesn't really want to take any initiative on his way out the door, though he has been talking about retiring for about ten years.

Strangely, the one person who was most concerned with our lack of progress during that time was Walt, I think because he shines most in his doomsday role when things are getting done. However, as soon as Aidon stopped being the chair of the committee, Walt started complaining that things had gotten worse. Even more than that, he joined the GOD squad. Despite the name, the GOD squad has nothing to do with religion, though its adherents are every bit as faithful as—if not more faithful than—those who are first to occupy the pews on Sunday morning. GOD stands for the Good Old Days squad, and they hold fast to the "fact" that everything was so great in the past but is so bad now. (I must admit, I may soon join this group, especially with all the recent "improvements.") This stance fits Walt's worldview perfectly, but he is not the only one. Walt, Train, and Claude are all members of the GOD squad for this committee, though when they start on one of their nostalgic sermons, Claude only manages to make inappropriate jokes, like when our committee was assigned to do a "hot wash" after the emergency fire drill disaster, and Claude kept referring to it as "ball wash." He generally is the only one who laughs at his own jokes, but he *is* a survivor. This is demonstrated by the fact that he is still here, given that everyone is offended by everything and even if someone isn't, somebody else will be offended for them. NuPol refers to them as the EOB group, Eternally Offended on others' Behalf. Someone heard him say that out loud one time, and of course, they were offended. But he is NuPol, so he survived.

Taliban finally spoke up with a safety share. "One time, I was getting my kid's football off the roof because it was stuck behind the chimney. I just used my step ladder and heaved myself up there, but once I got the football, I realized that my stepladder was a few feet below my roof. I wasn't sure how I could get down."

Train interrupted. "You raise a good point. Offsite safety is vital, especially since we are the agency's greatest asset." (He always says crap like that, which is why I think they keep rewarding him by sending him to training.) But he wasn't finished. "You know, we really need training on offsite safety related to household tasks. If employees develop that mentality at home, they will bring that vigilance to work, and we will all be safer." I could see his wheels turning as he grabbed his pencil and started writing on a notepad.

He is the only one who seems to still use pencils, which he must bring from home, and risk brain impairment. Train can't say Walt didn't warn him. I'm sure this will result in more training for Train so that he can come back and train the trainers throughout the agency, which in reality means we will never hear about this subject again once he goes to training for it.

Claude piped up. "Boy, talk about getting high. Good thing we don't do random drug testing anymore." He laughed; Vi smiled awkwardly and then looked back at Taliban.

"That must have been scary," Vi said. "How did you get down, Taliban?"

"Well, I leaned over the edge and kept sliding, little by little, feeling with my toes to see if I could make contact with the ladder." True to his name, Taliban then went on for several minutes talking about the last ladder he'd bought because his old wooden one had too much paint on it and how he had a coupon but they didn't honor it and he had to come back the next day when the manager was there and, well, a bunch of other things I didn't capture because I zoned out when I heard something about a tree branch being in the road and the bank close to his house closing early. It was a valuable safety share, and I regretted that I wasn't able to pay closer attention as my mind wandered back to the problems in my own office.

Vi snapped me out of my stupor. "Well, as you all know, the DRIP subcommittee has been given the important task of reviewing if the button on the left side of our new commodes should be for number one or number two. It seems there has been some confusion, even with the pictures we suggested they add from our previous meeting." I noticed her seriousness when she said the words "important task."

I didn't put in a toilet discussion warning here because with

Claude, every meeting should probably come with that. But our important DRIP subcommittee task was about toilets. By the way, DRIP stands for Delegation for Risk Identification and Planning.

Train started the thoughtful analysis by framing the issue in some corporate-speak he likely got at some development program. "So what we need to do is ensure that our people obtain and maintain their critical skills. Whatever solution we decide, we need to make sure we have a good package of options to present to management and recommend the most feasible and equitable solution."

I saw Vi shoot him a dirty look. I have seen the unstated tension between these two before, and also Taliban. It's because the niches they have carved out for themselves—Train spouting corporate-speak, Vi spouting the obvious, and Taliban talking a lot about nothing—often overlap. There are nuances of differences in the critical roles that they each play, but I agree with NuPol's take on this: The common tie between them is that they have the valuable skill of being able to speak a lot but do not really say anything. They are perfect government employees, however, as every nuance of an issue needs to be reviewed ad nauseam, especially after a final decision is made.

Claude jumped to attention. "Well, if we are exploring options, maybe we need to require people to use the bathroom before they come into work, and that way, we won't even need bathrooms here." He chuckled, but no one else did. The others were actually nodding their heads and reflecting pensively. (Nod to word-of-the-day calendar.)

Walt sighed. "We can't just tell people not to have bowel movements at work. And we can't have this confusing system in place. Think of left-handed people, forgodsake. (He said this as one word as spit flew out of his mouth. He was full of passion and on a roll.) Think of people on the spectrum and how they might interpret signs and placards. We are asking our people to work in terrible conditions. This can't be a sweatshop. We must demand reasonable accommodations now!"

This reality even shut Claude down. No one spoke. Then Vi took charge. "I see we are up against the time. We need to set up the next meeting date. Everybody, look at your calendars."

Phones came out of pockets, and daily planners were opened. I looked at Train's and saw a series of trainings scheduled for the rest of the week. I heard him exhale out his nose in an exaggerated way and mumble under his breath, "Ah, this is so hard."

I also saw that Taliban didn't have anything written on his planner for the month, except this DRIP meeting. Maybe his world revolves around this meeting, and that's why he talks so much. His expansive reflections generally take up the whole meeting.

Then there was the eternally puzzling process of determining the time for the next meeting, with everyone's voices overlapping:

"How about the fifteenth of next month?"

"Ahhh, can't do that. I see on my calendar it is a Swahili holiday."

Nods all around.

"How about the seventeenth?"

"Hmm, that's around the budget delivery time. We may not have the bandwidth to do both."

Nods.

"How about the next Monday?"

"Uh, there is a Washington Commanders game the Sunday before, so people will want to watch that."

Nods.

"How about Thursday of that week?"

There was almost agreement and then, "Oh, shoot, we forgot:

Middle East Heritage Day. We are going to have a speaker in the main auditorium."

"How about that Friday?" That one came from Train, but all heads except his shook *no*, alongside a chorus of "No Fridays" or some such variation.

"Then how about the next Tuesday?"

"No, that's a Jewish holiday."

"The next day, Wednesday?"

No nods or protests. Everybody looked up.

"That Wednesday it is," Vi said, sounding satisfied.

I have to say, Vi ran a great meeting. We showed up, restated the problem we had been working on for months, got a reminder from Walt of the terrible consequences of both fixing and not fixing it, and then dutifully planned the next meeting while taking into account the sensibilities of every conceivable group we could imagine, even though no one in the meeting was from any of those groups. The meeting had been a huge success, and there was no reason to focus on something insignificant like the fact that nothing was really accomplished.

15

A Guru's Devolution and a Reflection on BLOGE

I met with Effing G three times, and each time, I got the feeling that he cared less and less about my improvement projects. The first time, I was supposed to go to his office, but a few minutes beforehand, he sent a message to say we could do a call instead. In the message, he asked me to remind him what we were meeting about, and I replied that it was related to progress on my journal, my attitude toward the efficiency improvements, and my thoughts on how I could contribute.

I didn't dare mention the community service fiasco and was praying it didn't come up. However, last night, I thought about a potential solution if it did. Maybe I could ask my buddy Chris to sign the paper showing that I had completed it, since he is an officer on the alumni board, provided he isn't still mad at me for being responsible for his parking lot beating. It was either that or I forge Alex's signature, but I dismissed that thought as soon as it appeared, as I was certain she would find out and I would be crucified, or something even worse.

He rang my number, and I picked up with a "hello."

"Oh, oh, yeah, thanks for reminding me. The journal. How is that going?" Effing G said, getting straight to the point.

I sat up in my chair, ultra-paranoid that he could see me slouching through the phone. I was well aware that this guy held my fate in his hands, at least related to my career. I even put on a fake smile, hoping that showed through the phone. "It's going great. I really wish I had started keeping a journal a long time ago."

I didn't hear anything for a few seconds and wondered if I had lost him. Then I heard faint clicking in the background and wondered if he was consulting some checklist of things he was supposed to ask me. When he said nothing, I decided to fill the dead time with my own enthusiastic advocacy for the initiative, which I secretly hoped would convince him that the brief time I'd spent pouring my feelings into the journal had already changed me and he would say I could stop.

"This has really been a boost to my attitude. I see more clearly now how important it is to reflect on how things are going and how each of us plays an important role in driving toward a more efficient work environment." As soon as I said this last sentence, I was kind of afraid I had pushed it too far and that he could see through my reverse-psychology strategy. That, and I almost threw up in my own mouth thinking about how much like Buzz and Train I sounded.

The typing continued, uninterrupted, and I thought I heard him mumble something to someone in the background. After a few more seconds, the typing stopped, and he came back on the line.

"Oh, uh, good work environment. Yeah, that's important." He also seemed to use the trick of simply commenting on the last words someone said to give the impression he had listened to the whole conversation. I thought I had invented that.

"I'm sorry, remind me again, what are we meeting about?" he asked.

At this point, I knew my reverse psychology had been for naught.

"My journal," I replied.

"Oh, yes, how is that going?"

"It's going great," I added, deciding not to waste my breath by extolling the virtues of the assignment and how it had led me out of the wilderness and into the light.

"Okay, that sounds good. Continue doing it, and we'll talk more at our next meeting. I'll send an invite." After a brief pause, he added, "Was there anything else you wanted to discuss?" The monotone clicking resumed.

"Uh, no, I'm fine, thank you." I hung up after we traded good-byes. I didn't want to prolong the conversation, concerned that the whole community service aspect would arise, but I almost felt like I was bothering him by attending the mandatory meeting that he'd set up.

The second meeting was much the same. It was put on the calendar as an in-person meeting in his office, but he sent a message about a half hour before it started, indicating that we would be doing it by phone again. He seemed similarly preoccupied during the second meeting, with the continuous typing and the background conversation. However, when it got to the point where he asked if there was anything else I wanted to discuss, I timidly asked a question I didn't really want to ask but felt I needed to know.

"I'm keeping my journal, and it is going well. Do you think you will want to see it at some point?"

The clicking continued but slowed as, I assume, he was thinking about an answer. "Uh, see it?" he asked, as if he had not thought about that before. "No, I don't think that's necessary. But continue to keep it. It's very important."

I'd assured him that I would and thanked him for the call, though I don't even think he said bye before hanging up.

For the third meeting, there was no pretense it would be in person. The invite just said, "I'll call" for the location. Right off the bat, he mentioned he was running up against another meeting, so we would keep this one short. He continued to appear distracted while we went through the motions, but when he got to his check-the-box question, if there was anything else I would like to discuss, I decided to ask the big one.

"May I ask what is happening with the workforce? I mean, we've been through three rounds of Deferred Resignation, Voluntary Retirement, and RIFs. Are there more layoffs or downsizing efforts planned?" I knew it was bold of me to ask, since the issue of layoffs, buyouts, and all other downsizing efforts was forbidden in any conversation, but I thought that if another round was on the way, he would know that sooner than I would.

I heard a big inhale on the other end of the phone and a quick exhale. "We are taking any and all necessary actions to increase the efficiency of federal agencies. That's what the taxpayers demand, and it is what we intend to do. Any news of that sort will clearly be communicated by the Office of Personnel Management and by each agency head or their designee." I could tell he was just reading this, and his smug corporate-speak response provided no information that I didn't already know and left no room for follow-up. I knew it was time to go.

"Um," he added after a slight pause. "By the way, I'm changing the frequency of these meetings to an as-needed basis from now on. Don't assume we will have it if you don't get an invite directly from me."

"I understand. Minimizing unnecessary meetings is very efficient," I added, hearing the sickening sucking sound in my own voice.

It was to no avail. He simply forced out an "Uh-huh" on the other end. Then he added, "Well, if that's all, we're finished."

I thanked him and hung up the phone. I couldn't help but think my impromptu question about future layoffs may have caught him off guard and caused him to cancel, or at least rethink, our future meetings. So while I didn't get an answer to my question, maybe it served the purpose of getting me out of these regular check-ins, which I still dreaded even though they seemed to be getting less and less important to him anyway.

Or maybe I *did* get an answer. I think if the answer was a definite "no," he might have said that, so essentially, I need to be prepared for more turmoil with the workforce. And since it seems he doesn't care about seeing my journal anytime soon, maybe I can be a little bolder and reflect on how I really feel about this whole BLOGE efficiency push, something I haven't really allowed myself to do in-depth yet. Besides, if worse comes to worst, and we do have an in-person meeting in the future, I can just rip the next few pages out of my journal and swear I don't know what happened to them. So here goes.

When the current administration decided to clean house across the federal agencies, some people were strongly opposed to the idea, and a few were strongly in favor of it. I, like most others, took a wait-and-see approach. Most of us have worked through bureaucratic changes before, and we have always tried our best to do what they want and go with the flow. However, from the beginning, this felt different. There had been a lot of talk of this new efficiency group, BLOGE, which would sort of be like a government agency, but not really. Then opinion pieces began appearing in major newspapers saying things that federal employees had never heard before, like we were ripping off the taxpayers because a lot of us worked remotely.

A few employees started circulating clips in emails with messages of doom and gloom, but they were generally the employees who always preach doom and gloom (you better believe Walt was involved), so most of us figured those articles were written by outliers and that those in power knew we were dedicated to our jobs and the mission of our agency.

Although we thought we might be working on new initiatives, we assumed our jobs would basically continue just as they were. Many of us were still working from home after the pandemic, and, in fact, a lot of people had been hired with an explicit remote agreement as part of their onboarding package because the organization had determined their jobs could be done from anywhere if they had a computer and could log in. And it was true.

But one day, shortly after the change in administration, we got a cryptic email that, at first glance, appeared to be spam and had a button at the bottom that said, "Reply." It appeared to be from the Office of Personnel Management, or OPM. Apparently, most people were like me and assumed it was spam, as our IT department has routinely scolded us for clicking on links from strange emails. Then, we got a second email from the same address telling us that the first email wasn't spam and that we needed to reply.

But again, most of us pretty much figured that is what a spammer would do, so we ignored it again. But then we all got snail mail letters in our mailboxes from HR on agency letterhead, telling us that the emails weren't spam and that we should reply. But since we had deleted the emails thinking they were spam and blocked the sender, we had to write a letter back to HR telling them that we'd received the messages and didn't reply but that we *would* reply if we could figure out how to unblock the sender and recover the messages. So it was a rather, shall we say, inefficient process set up to let us know about the new efficiency initiative.

The next message that came to us said that we were at a fork in the road with our careers, and they needed to cut costs by getting rid of a bunch of us useless bureaucrats who barely worked anyway. I'm paraphrasing, but that is generally what it said. There was also a strange (and very long) page talking about how those who stayed were going to have to start actually working and how there were others who were simply hopeless and would be forced to leave. We were supposed to sign that we understood these scenarios (and, presumably, agreed with them), though many of us thought we were *already* working and didn't want to leave.

Another peculiar part said that a nongovernmental government department was going to cut costs and get rid of the waste in government. But if we weren't committed to improving ourselves, we could resign, and they would pay us to sit home doing nothing for six months until they could officially get our useless asses off their financial books—or we could go part time and train high school interns to do our jobs. Again, I'm paraphrasing. Believe it or not, these options were not highly motivating to the workforce; in fact, there was more confusion than motivation.

None of the supervisors knew what was happening, and when people asked the HR department in our agency if this whole thing was serious, no one in HR knew, even the higher-level managers. They said we needed to check the Frequently Asked Questions on the OPM website, which essentially said this was a legitimate offer and that those people who wanted to sit at home and keep ripping off taxpayers could just take this great deal and go on a vacation. The unions representing many federal employees said that it was not legitimate and that we should ignore it, which most of us did.

Then they saw fit to sweeten the pot and offered to let employees retire early and get paid even longer to sit at home and do nothing (or go on vacation) and start drawing our pensions earlier. We were still confused, and judges started stepping in ruling that the offer might not be legal, but some more employees took the deal, though apparently not enough. They wanted to purge 10% of the workforce, and they weren't even close at that point.

So then they started the reductions in force, or RIFs. They started with the low-hanging fruit, those on probation, meaning they were high performers who came from somewhere else, and though we wanted them in the government, they had the misfortune of being hired in the last couple of years. Also, the people who were hired to work remotely as a way to get the best talent, with the benefit of letting people work from home, were next. They also started firing people who had not responded to the confusing series of emails mentioned earlier, even though many heads of agencies (appointees of this same administration) told their employees to ignore those emails.

Then they put in a performance test. We all had to download an app and take a test that tracked our time and flagged us if we didn't type 100 words per minute. Fortunately, the software had a flaw and only measured time, not quality, so most of us figured out to just bang out nonsense on our keyboards, and we were fine. Some of the more honest employees tried to actually do it, and few of them could, so they were gone. That was the real benefit—they were able to get rid of the most honest employees. Then other people were RIFed because their entire department had been slashed. There were multiple rounds of this cycle, with judges intervening each time to delay the offer, only to have higher courts stay the delay, giving employees days or hours to accept the latest offer. It is really hard to see why we feds were confused about anything in this seamless, efficient process.

It was against this background that I was introduced to the whole efficiency effort. Of course, in Washington, DC, whether it is a piece of legislation, a program, or even this pseudo-government department, which is not really a part of the government at all, everything has a name that makes it hard to oppose. Even this Bureau for Logistics Optimization and General Efficiency—who could oppose that? I cannot blame them for naming it this. How many people would support the Department of Slash the Shit out of the Federal Workforce and We'll Figure Out What to Do Later? That doesn't even make a good acronym.

Maybe being exposed to the rollout this way is what caused me and most federal employees I know to have a bad reaction to this initiative. Now let me be clear. I, like most federal employees, am all for cutting waste and fraud and gaining efficiency. Most of us don't like waste any more than any other taxpayer does. In fact, there is waste and we know it, and if we were empowered to, most of us would be delighted to help get rid of it and improve our processes. But unfortunately, this effort seemed to be only about haphazardly cutting headcount and not trying to strategically get rid of waste.

For example, the salary of all government employees combined is only about 4% of the annual federal budget, so they could fire every single one of us, and it wouldn't make a noticeable dent in the national debt. Also, there were many issues that hurt the credibility of the efficiency effort. We were told that BLOGE (and later names that it would try to adopt, though we all still knew it as BLOGE) was composed of the smartest financial minds in the world and that they were using the latest artificial intelligence tools, so there would be no mistakes. But there were mistakes. Oh, so many. For example, in the Department of Energy, they eliminated the office that facilitates exchanges of energy to grids in the northeast, including the Washington, DC, area. One of my friends who works there said that they were sitting at work one day and the lights went out, leaving everyone wondering what happened. It's a sad state of affairs when the Department of Energy can't pay its power bill.

In another mishap, one of the premises of the downsizing was that national security would not be affected. However, BLOGE fired several people who worked at the National Nuclear Security Administration, which maintains the nuclear stockpile. The brilliant minds from Silicon Valley, using the latest AI tools, couldn't figure out that an agency with "National Nuclear Security" in its name might have something to do with national security. Mishaps like these left many agencies scrambling to rehire people who were fired, only to inform them shortly thereafter that they were fired again because they hit another criterion.

In summary, I am all for making the government more efficient. But I feel there was a much more—dare I say—efficient way to do that. It's kind of like the shared drive at work. It's built on a good idea, but the way ours was rolled out and implemented was an unmitigated disaster.

The normal attrition rate from the federal government is around 6% each year. If they had only put in place a hiring freeze, in two years, they would have far exceeded their 10% goal, and people wouldn't be in constant fear of losing their jobs or making a wrong move. Now it's a toxic environment, and everyone is afraid to do anything, for fear they may do it wrong and have a target on their back. So we have apparently made the government more efficient by indiscriminately getting rid of people and creating an environment where their only defense is being inefficient and not taking any initiative.

Anyway, back to pretending to get back to the grind.

16

Offsite Therapy: Nextdoor

I have felt super wiped out the last few days when I've gotten home. I come in the door, plop down on the couch, and mindlessly surf channels until I go wake up the computer. I really don't know why I'm so drained. Maybe it's the meetings, or the added responsibility of being the boss, or that NuPol is now my adversary, or a combination of all these.

It seems Reima is wiped out too. She works as a government contractor, mostly doing translations. Her company has some contracts with private companies too, so she has been able to survive the contract funding massacre. We each have our respites. Hers seems to be finding juicy TV series in Spanish on one of the streaming services we have. I never know which one, so I keep them all. I'm just glad they grab the money from my account before I ever see it so I never really miss it. My respite, especially as of late, has definitely become Nextdoor.

Many people will immediately know what I am talking about. It is a social media app that is supposed to bring communities together. However, it seems to do that only by letting people who are eternally outraged vent at each other. I kind of think that all the HOA presidents, people who were tattletales as children, and people who felt wronged about anything at any point in their life got together and created Nextdoor. It is a fabulous invention, and mere words cannot express the joy it has brought me as of late to watch the virtual ping-pong matches. Oh, there is one group I left out that also loves to participate in Nextdoor therapy: those who enjoy messing with the people who are the admins on Nextdoor.

When I see that there is a post with, say, 196 replies, that means it is a good one, ripe with comments. The most I ever saw was 324 before the whole thread was shut down by the admins. That time, it was about some idiot lawmaker in Richmond, Virginia's capital, who had introduced a bill to build a casino in our district. Not in his district, of course. He lives just west of Middleburg, which was a retreat for John and Jackie Kennedy and John Warner and Elizabeth Taylor when they were married. (Yes, she was married to a US Senator at one time, and as many times as she was married, it's surprising she didn't collect a number of Congressmen in her net, but I digress.) Now, a gaudy casino would never do around Middleburg, where the rolling hills are adorned with polo fields, wineries, old stone fences, and quaint restaurants owned by Hollywood types who retired to this enclave of paradise. This lawmaker had to propose building a casino in our district.

That thread went on and on between those who argued about the economic benefits that could come from a casino (which largely includes those who will adamantly defend whatever those in authority say) and those who talk about how much a casino would "gunk up" our beautiful community. Now, I like our community, but a quaint and charming neighborhood it is not. For that, we go to Old Town Alexandria, or we venture across the bridge and go to Georgetown. That long thread was only stopped when someone called the politician a douche, and then a social media brawl broke out about what exactly a douche was, and was it an offensive word or just a benign descriptor, and if it is slanderous to ever speak ill of a diligent politician doing his best in Richmond. I followed that thread for three days, and then, sadly, it was taken down one day when I was at work, so I never saw the final ruling on what, exactly, constitutes a douche.

That evening after work, I went into my makeshift office that doubles as a spare bedroom when Reima's family comes to town. I shook the mouse to wake up my computer (which I never turn off), sat back in my worn chair with tape wrapped around the armrests to keep the foam from coming out, cracked my knuckles, and opened the email notifying me of a new post. I clicked on the link. People were typing, so I got to see the action in real time, and I was mad at myself for not getting a drink first. I wasn't going to leave this show for something as unnecessary as food or drinks, so I settled in like a Greek citizen in ancient Olympia observing the parade of athletes.

When you log onto Nextdoor and see one of these free-for-alls in real time, you must have a strategy to get the most effect. When I was a novice, I foolishly went to the real-time conversation and followed that, figuring I could go back later and catch up on the backstory. But as I matured to my higher level as master observer, I realized that was the wrong approach. You see, sometimes people respond to a comment that happened ten or fifteen posts ago, so while I know someone is mad or trying to make someone else feel stupid or evil, I don't really know what they are talking about.

I went through a period when I started at the beginning of the thread and diligently read each post, trying to match later outrage posts with earlier tantalizing ones, but it was not always easy. And besides, the conversation usually seemed to peter out by the time I got caught up, and then it was devoid of outrage (or comments were removed). So I would be in a bad mood the rest of the night, having missed the real-time energy.

That is when I developed my current approach, a hybrid method, which I truly think is the best of both worlds. I now go back and forth. I go to the very first post to see what started it; then I go to the most up-to-date post to see what the current outrage is. Then I go back to the beginning and read a few old ones, then a few newer ones, and seesaw back and forth until I'm up to date. But I do make sure to stop on the posts of my favorite participants.

People are supposed to use their real names, but since there are names like Chicken Nugget Five, Land Sakes, and Baked Tofu, I'm almost positive some people have figured out how to use aliases. I enjoy them all, but my two favorites are at it tonight: End Cruelty and Blow Hole 7. These two argue so much, they could be married. Maybe they are. Tonight's episode is about foxes. Apparently, End Cruelty (EC) started the post by saying that foxes were nesting and people should leave them alone. Then Blow Hole 7 (BH7) countered by asking how many foxes it took to make a decent coat. EC indicated disgust and noted that the mama was just taking care of her kits. (Apparently, a baby fox is called a kit; good to know.) Then BH7 pondered how tasty baby kit meat must be because they haven't toughened up yet. Then EC expressed the hope that BH7 would be attacked by a giant fox that would barbecue BH7 on a grill. (I guess ending cruelty has exceptions.) Then BH7 asked who would win in a fight between a mama fox and a rabid pit bull. At that point, Land Sakes stepped in like a dutiful peacemaker and suggested that maybe the conversation should be taken offline and it would not be good to see two of God's simple creatures fighting just because the circumstances put them together, to which BH7 said that EC was not one of God's innocent creatures but remnants of the brief period of time when the devil took over the world and tried his own hand at creation and that's why we have such gnarly creatures as mean foxes, hedgehogs, and EC. At this, Chicken Nugget Five decided to weigh in and stick up for hedgehogs, to which Baked Tofu took great offense that hedgehogs were being singled out with no just cause.

I rocked back in my chair as my arm rubbed the armrest tape, making a squeaking sound. There was no way I was leaving this, but I had to have some popcorn. I yelled to the TV room for Reima to please make me some popcorn but heard a string of what I assume were expletives in Spanish that ended in words that sounded like "el climax," "novela," and "stupido gringo." I decided I didn't really need the popcorn after all.

After several more rounds online, I was exhausted, and as I heard the credits roll in the other room, I walked in right as Reima yawned.

"Ready for bed?" I asked. She nodded, and we both trundled off to the bedroom, scooting our feet along and walking slowly like two old boxers who were past their prime and had barely survived the fight. It had been a good evening for both of us. She fell asleep and snored a faint little sound that I would have thought was cute if I didn't know it was a snore, before I drifted off to thoughts of my own boxing ring.

17

My Legacy: The Shared Drive, Part 1

I dragged myself into work the next day, still feeling the fatigue of watching the enthralling virtual cage match the night before. There was another episode of NuPol not showing up on time, Mini and Negativa Diva waiting by the elevator to ask me what I was going to do about it, and Buzz stopping in my office for an hour and a half to tell me how busy he was and how he couldn't cram anything else into his day.

This time, Buzz was talking about his dog, Trix, spelled with an *x*, which he always added as if I had not heard the spelling a thousand times before. Apparently, Trix was feeling low because Buzz was so busy at work and so tired when he got home. Honestly, I wondered if Trix was just tired of Buzz and his stupid tangents about how important he was and how much he was doing and decided to play sick so he would just shut up. But I think dogs are better than that. They are better than humans. They pretend to care, no matter how stupid their humans are.

Buzz kept going on about how he thinks maybe Trix needs therapy and how hard it must be for her living with such a hard-working human. He also talked about how he has to leave Trix with a neighbor when he travels and how that must traumatize her. As he spoke, I looked at him, really looked at him, for a minute. I noticed his reddish, puffy cheeks, the hint of lines running from the corners of his eyes, and his broad but unsure, almost boyish face. For a minute, I felt sorry for Buzz. He seems to desperately want people, and apparently his dog, to think he is indispensable. I guess that is how he gets his meaning in life. He feels he is indispensable, and for the niche that he has carved out, I guess in a way he is. My heart softened for a moment as I reflected on this, and then he laughed a forced laugh, as if amused by his observation that no one else was enlightened enough to understand, and I was snapped back to reality. He may have a sad backstory, and he may embellish his role as a not-so-subtle cry for help, but he was still an annoying shit.

I tried all the tricks with Buzz: not making eye contact, picking up the phone to make a call, trying the old "Oh, shoot, I forgot I had to do something" routine, but nothing fazed old Buzz. Finally, I said I had to go to the meeting with More of Less, and though I was forty-five minutes early, I stood up and walked toward the elevator, with Buzz in tow, mentioning some ideas he had about how to make the office more efficient. I pushed the button at the elevator just in time for Mini and Negativa Diva to show up. "What about NuPol? He's still not here?" they squawked, though I could barely hear them over Buzz's debrief.

The bell dinged, and as the elevator door opened, I had a stroke of genius. "I'm on my way to the meeting. Why don't the three of you discuss the NuPol situation while I'm gone?" They all three looked at me with bewilderment. This was not the normal look of disdain from Negativa Diva, mirrored by Mini, or the lost, longing puppy look that Buzz usually gave if he was cut off from discussing how busy he was. It was genuine bewilderment. As the door was closing, I held it open with my hand and added, "And please have Buzz discuss his latest tasks with you two." The bewilderment was coupled with wide eyes as the door closed, and I was alone. I was getting the hang of this.

At More of Less's meeting, it was more of the same, though because of an email from the Secretary relating the latest injunction from a judge, we didn't have to promote DEI but had to take action to ensure that people from traditionally marginalized groups did not feel disenfranchised. The attorneys were apparently figuring out the difference, but in the meantime, we were to choose a marginalized community and explore our unconscious bias toward them. We started with an awareness share led by the Director of Appreciation, who was dressed in a big cat costume, apparently representing the Furry community, which I've learned (don't ask me how) is a larger subculture than you'd think. We were asked to take a moment and discuss how we have been insensitive to someone we considered the "other," and when there were no takers, we were asked to close our eyes and reflect on the negative energy we were creating by not owning up to our failings, and how the cat could now tell that we were uncomfortable with having a cat in our meeting even if we didn't know it.

The one thing I got out of it was when More of Less talked about how the job was about more than our "temporal actions"— how we needed to consider our legacy. As I was trying to think to myself over the purring, it came to me what my legacy should be: destroying the dreaded shared drive.

Now, I touched briefly on my feelings about the shared drive, but I want to be clear why I feel so strongly about it. I usually go with the flow and find the path of least resistance. But there is one thing I despise with a passion, and it is the shared drive. I've hated the stupid shared drive since we first started using it. I don't hate the idea of it; that actually makes sense. It was sold to us as a place where we could collect all our documents, such as they are, and we could all collaborate on them simultaneously. It was supposed to kick our productivity into overdrive. That is what we were told. It would "turbocharge" our co-creative juices.

Right off the bat, I saw a problem. We never work together anyway, so I wasn't sure why we had to find a way to make a more efficient process for something we never do. But after the protestations of everyone on staff, we use it, except NuPol, who got a waiver because it triggered him, and Negativa Diva, who got a waiver because she complained so much and wore Less down. So it basically boils down to Mini, Buzz, and I all trying to figure out how to make this thing work.

The problems really started from the beginning with the roll-out. They put all of us, including Less, in a training room with a table and computers around the desk in front of each of us. The older Santa Claus–looking guy from IT bragged about how he had been connecting people online since the '90s. He was supposed to walk us through how to link to the shared drive, which they called mapping. Our individual drives would still be there for us to keep documents that we originated, but they were also supposed to map to this shared drive, which was going to be a vast improvement over the functioning and understandable way we have been doing things, which was to email files to someone if they needed to see them. Instead of mapping us all to the shared drive, though, apparently Santa Claus had mapped each of us to the individual drive of someone else. Mine mapped to Mini's, and unfortunately for Less, Negativa Diva's mapped to his. She started reading all his messages out loud, which were essentially that he felt we were untrainable and the worst staff he had ever dealt with.

I'm not sure whose drive Buzz saw, but it seemed like he was happy because when he saw the tasks from whomever it was, he started taking notes and mumbling things like, "That's a good one."

Imagine the chaos. We were all together in this room. Santa Claus knew '90s networks like the hair in his beard but apparently didn't grasp how to handle today's networks. Negativa Diva was reading Less's messages aloud, stopping to occasionally say, "This one is about you," as she pointed to someone and read something unflattering, including messages to General Counsel about NuPol. Upon hearing this, NuPol closed the lid on the laptop in front of him and said he needed to launch a protest since he had been disrespected, was offended, and would never do that to someone. (At this, my fingers froze above the keyboard, and I looked at him, trying hard not to snicker.)

With each new revelation, Mini was looking at Negativa Diva admiringly, like a teenager on a first date, or kind of like, I imagine, Moses looking at the Ten Commandments he received on Mount Sinai. To occupy myself, I read through some of Mini's emails, almost all of which were to Negativa Diva, bragging on how brave Negativa Diva was and how she had showed "him" during the meeting (hard to know which "him" she meant, since Negativa Diva gives everyone a hard time).

After about ten minutes, Less finally demanded that Santa Claus fix the situation, which he did by inadvertently deleting everything that any of us had in our emails and individual shared drives. And I mean *really* deleting—never to be recovered again. After that, Less admonished each of us for not having backups of our material on flash drives, which we had been told never to do and which was supposedly unnecessary because our individual drives and the shared drive would protect our information forever and were constantly backed up. There was apparently a different reality, as IT said they didn't do that and didn't intend to, citing security concerns, which they never explained. Less sent a carefully worded email out to the staff, reminding us how important it was to protect our information, which was ultimately the property of the taxpayers. The email also reminded us that we were not to use any flash drives, which we should have done to preserve our data.

Our introduction to the shared drive only went downhill from there. It is unavailable most of the time, and we found out that it only selectively saves changes. Every time we edit a document, we are told not to assume that the change is saved but to print out a copy so that we can go line by line to compare what changed. All these extra steps, which were unnecessary before, are apparently how we have improved our efficiency. It is still a mystery to me how the efficiency gurus, who invaded our federal spaces a few months ago, and about whom we were told were the best and smartest in the world using the latest technology to leave no stone unturned in seeking out inefficiencies, have failed to identify and immediately obliterate this stain on the consciousness of productivity that we call the shared drive. After the discussion about legacy in More of Less's meeting, I am determined to change that.

First, I sent an email to the IT help desk, copying my staff, requesting that they change the system for our office, dispense with the shared drive, and go back to having only individual drives, which each person controls themselves. When I hit Send, I felt a real sense of accomplishment. Even if I did nothing else during my tenure as boss, I would destroy the shared drive. I tilted my head back and closed my eyes. The staff would love me, and I would do something to help the department. I envisioned the staff putting up a framed picture of me with a placard talking about how I single-handedly took on this terrible organizational menace. For several minutes, I sat that way, listening to the air flow in and out of my nostrils. I was at peace. This must be how it felt to win a Nobel Prize. Maybe I would get special recognition from the Secretary's office. Getting rid of the shared drive would be my legacy, and what a proud legacy to have.

I walked out of my office with more pep in my step. Mini was waiting by the elevator, uncharacteristically without Negativa Diva, and said, "NuPol came in for a while but left early."

I wanted to ignore the comment but said, "I'll talk to him. By the way, where is Negativa Diva?"

"She had to coordinate with Buzz on something but wanted to make sure I let you know the seriousness of the situation."

I thought that was odd. Negativa never coordinates with anybody except Mini to control her every action, but I let it go with a quick, "Okay."

That evening at home, I opened Nextdoor. It is like a drug I cannot stop. End Cruelty and Blow Hole 7 were at it again, leading their respective factions. Apparently, someone was walking their dog, and they put, shall we say, its business in End Cruelty's garbage can by the curb. EC was livid that someone would throw crap in her bin without her consent, but BH7 countered that EC probably had things in the garbage much worse than the dog poop and asked if that was the real issue. But there was another player today—one who said he had taken a break but was back again. One who went by My Chance. My Chance (MC) apparently was not allied with either faction and was making no effort to join them. MC said that both EC and BH7 should jump in the garbage with the dog crap because that's where they belonged. At this, an administrator jumped in and stopped the thread while distributing the rules governing participation again. That was fine with me. Actually, I wasn't in the mood to watch the online train-wreck tonight. I walked into the TV room and asked Reima if she wanted to go to dinner. She looked up from her novela, surprised, and said, "Uh, oh, okay. You don't want to order delivery?"

"Not tonight. Let's celebrate."

"Celebrate what?" she asked.

"My legacy," I responded with a smile.

"Your what?" she asked, tilting her head to one side like a confused puppy.

"Never mind," I replied. "Let's just say I'm making the world better. Feel like Italian?"

18

Slug for a Day

My joy withstood the mediocre Italian meal with cold lasagna that we sent back (which we never do), a small scuffle with Reima over what to watch on TV in bed (she wanted Spanish and I wanted English, so we compromised on something in Turkish that neither of us understood or liked, and so we fell asleep early), and apparently sleeping wrong with my head on both pillows (as opposed to my normal procedure of sleeping on one and using the other to cover my ear while my head is tilted to the side) and the ensuing neck cramps the next morning. Nothing was going to rain on my parade today. I had my legacy to think about.

I was feeling bold, like a general ready to walk through a field to watch my opponent surrender and present his sword to me, holding it out with both hands like a tray. If the shared drive was a person, it would do that. In fact, I was feeling so empowered that I decided to do something I never do.

My commute generally consists of waiting in a line, getting on a bus, moving toward the back of the bus because there are no seats left, standing and swaying, and almost falling at least once on the fifteen-minute ride to the train station, where I catch the train for a twenty-minute ride to DC. Then, when I arrive at my stop, I zigzag fifteen more minutes to my office, mindlessly walking against the light at intersections.

However, a warrior turned general with a legacy to pursue doesn't stand and sway against his will and zigzag and almost get killed on his way to the battlefield. A warrior turned general rides in glory to the battlefield, propped up erect on the back of a gold-studded chariot with red tassels hanging off the sides, occasionally removing his gladiator hat to let his impressive but thinning dirty blond mane flow in the wind. Since there are no chariots at my bus stop, I turned my gaze to the Slug Line.

I will explain this for my senile self's sake, who may read this one day in the future and wonder what I was talking about. The Slug Line is a fascinating phenomenon that, as far as I know, only officially exists in DC. It may sound like something nasty, but the Slug Line is a revered tradition, and there is often much competition for it. Cars cannot go into DC during the rush hours in the express lanes unless they have at least three passengers. So to get around this problem, people line up at various bus stops to get the chance to ride in a car with others they don't know to be dropped off at an unknown destination. It is a regal chance to ride in style, get to the office much quicker, and, best of all, not stand and sway on a bus.

When I first moved here, I recoiled at the thought of either Reima or me getting into a car with strangers and being driven to some unknown destination in Washington, DC. I started to hear the Slugs, as the riders are called, talk around the proverbial water cooler about their commutes. (Note to self: Flip the page on the word-of-the-day calendar. I don't want to overuse "proverbial.") Over time, they developed their own elite group and referred to themselves as the Sluggers. They would talk about the official Slug rules, like not talking in the car, and how occasionally they would land a ride with a chatty Cathy (which could be of any sex or gender) who would share their exploits at their agency and the exotic places they were going that day, like to the National Mall or the Eisenhower Executive Building.

I evolved from being concerned to feeling that maybe I wasn't worthy of being a Slug. I guess I kind of had a Slug chip on my shoulder, and there's no worse feeling than a Slug on your back. It just became easier to keep the same commute routine, though I would occasionally look at the Slug Line and wonder how the other half lived. But not today. Warriors turned generals don't look and wonder; they see and conquer, and today this warrior turned general will be—I'm shaking with excitement as I write this—a Slug.

Now, Slugs aren't supposed to be choosy, but there is a bit of perceived prestige riding in nicer cars. It sometimes sounds like a car show around the cooler when the Sluggers start talking about their ride that day—either the newest version of the Mercedes, BMW, or Audi, or even an Alfa Romaro or Bentley. (Most Feds don't brag about riding in Teslas anymore.) It is proof that some government contractors or federal workers have learned to manage their money well, probably because Congress sets such a good example.

But anyway, I was next in line, and I closed my eyes, tilted my head back, and started tapping my foot with anticipation as to what style car I would ride in. I was picturing myself like a Roman general in a large-scale Ben Hur chariot when I heard a car horn, something I didn't think was allowed in the Slug Line. I opened my eyes and saw that my chariot had arrived: an old Honda that had so many bumper stickers it was hard to tell what color it was originally, though I figured that any original paint was long gone anyway.

"You coming?" asked a gruff voice with a small touch of femininity and a Michigan accent. I know accents because I am reminded of mine all the time in this "open-minded" city, and from just those two words, I could tell this one was from Michigan. There were three rapid taps on my shoulder, and the guy in the gray suit and blue tie behind me made a waving motion with his left arm to proceed to my chariot.

The back seat had an old quilt with strings of yarn tied in knots tucked into the corners, and the inside smelled like one of those medicinal shops you pass in downtown DC with the funny leaves drawn on the window. Without turning around, Ms. Michigan snapped, "We're stopping at the VA; that work for you?"

I cleared my throat as the mental image of my regal chariot was replaced with a homemade cardboard boxcar with wheels barely rolling. But a chariot is a chariot, and at least I wouldn't stand and sway on my way into DC today.

"Well?" Michigan asked, revving up the accelerator to a loud *whum, whum* sound that cars with bad mufflers make.

I cleared my throat. "That's fine. I work pretty close to there," I replied, reaching for the handle to roll down the window before noticing there was no knob. Michigan revved up the engine again, and off we went. Apparently, she had stopped at another bus stop earlier and picked up a Slug who had commandeered the shotgun seat. The first Slug looked like a young Willie Nelson type, complete with a long ponytail and colorful shirt.

The drive was going to feel a lot longer if we didn't talk, so I decided to break the Slug rules and strike up a conversation. "So how old is this car?" I blurted out, meaning it to be more conversational, though Ms. Michigan apparently took it as judgmental.

Michigan shot a look at young Willie as if she expected him to jump in, and I swallowed hard because I knew I was done for. I saw that look around DC a lot, and it was always followed by a sermon. "I know what you're thinking. You're thinking that this is an old gas guzzler, and I should get a newfangled electric car that they say is more environmentally friendly. Do you know what studies actually show about cars like that and how bad their whole life cycle is for the environment? Besides, how do you think changing out cars every two years helps in the long run? What happens to the old ones? Do you know what it takes to build a new car? Do you know how many people are exploited in the process? You sound like one of those people from the lily-white suburbs in Great Falls and McLean and Potomac and Bethesda who live far away from real people but close to other hypocrites like themselves so they can pull out their peckers in the form of the newest gadget that's supposed to save emissions while they fill up the landfills and . . ."

I was waiting for Michigan to take a breath so I could apologize, but it never came. I found out the only thing worse than sitting in silence is rousing this rare DC species. They work in DC trying desperately to make the world better, but they don't enrich themselves. They hate both political parties, and they are most sickened by those who criticize consumerism while demonstrating it. They drive old cars and recycle everything, live in modest communities in small houses, send their kids to public schools, and except for drug use, they generally obey the law. They live their values, but fortunately, there are so few people who actually do that in DC that I am usually not exposed to these sermons. I had a sighting today of this rare species. They are the True Believers.

I had zoned out several examples ago, but then Michigan stopped talking as if she was waiting for me to respond. She glared at me in the cracked rearview mirror, adjusting it to make sure I saw her, and young Willie turned and set his steely gaze on me. I swallowed hard and smiled and said the first thing that came to mind to break the silence. "What happened to the window knob?"

They stopped the car at the VA building and squeezed into a small parking spot that seemed to only exist because two big cars had encroached on either side. I wiggled out of the barely open car door, feeling exhausted, ashamed, upset, and humored all at the same time. But on the way to the office, what was important came back into mental view: Today might just be the day I slay the shared drive. My legacy.

19

The Memo: Take Two

I was both relieved and distressed when I got off the elevator. I was relieved because I didn't see Negativa Diva and Mini giving me a report on NuPol's schedule, and I didn't see Buzz eager to tell me all he was doing. But I was distressed to see someone I hadn't seen in a while: Uri.

"We need to talk. I'll follow you to your office," Uri said, sounding eager. I started walking, not responding, hoping maybe Buzz was waiting outside my door so I could get out of Uri's torment and subject myself to his instead.

I really don't know Uri very well, but his reputation precedes him. NuPol first encountered him a couple of years ago, when he was working on a procedure that—as I recall—NuPol himself likely instigated. I don't remember what the procedure was about, but I remember that Uri was somehow looped into the review cycle, and it got so bad that even NuPol, whose persistence is amazing when he thinks he can cause chaos, was ready to throw in the towel.

NuPol researched it and found out that nobody really knows who Uri is, where he came from, who he reports to, or what he does outside of reviews. All that is known is that he takes reviews to the extreme, finding every nit, and people get so frustrated that they just stop producing memos. NuPol theorizes that upper management loves Uri because he kills off products before they ever get to upper management, and therefore, management doesn't have to make a decision. NuPol is convinced it is deliberate and always works to their favor. If management should make a decision but doesn't, they can say they didn't know there was a problem and blame it on the person who initiated the memo but got worn out during Uri's endless review and didn't finish it. If something does come to management, they can always point to Uri's review and say that obviously the memo is so flawed that they are not ready to consider it. In other words, Uri is the one who kills off any incoming threat that may require management to actually do something. And he is uniquely gifted to do that. Most people hate to review those documents because even with new artificial intelligence tools that flag potential problems, they have to use actual intelligence to check the results. But Uri loves this. The name Uri fits him perfectly, because he loves to urinate on anything that anyone else produces, and I could tell by his expression that he had a full bladder and was ready to piss all over one of our memos.

"I hate to hit you right off the bat, but it's priority," he said, slapping the folder in his left hand with the back of his right one for emphasis. "I was going to take it up with the originator, but somebody from your office said he doesn't come in much anymore."

This memo must really be stressing Uri. I noticed his red tie had snaked down between his top and second button. Whenever I see him, he never looks disheveled in any way. He always has a black two-piece suit, white shirt, and a thin red tie. His gray-black hair is thinning and slicked back. He is always clean-shaven, and though he is short and wiry, that tie is always done up so tight that his head looks like a balloon tied with a red string. He must have noticed me looking because he slapped the folder on my desk and worked the knot back up against his neck.

After the necktie adjustment, he opened the folder, and I could see that it was NuPol's memo. I call it NuPol's memo because one of the last things Less did before leaving was to reassign the ASS memo to NuPol so I would have more time to supervise. I could see the memo had bright red all over it, matching Uri's tie. It looked like someone had brought a bucket from a slaughterhouse and slung it around mindlessly all over the memo. For a moment, I was concerned that maybe Uri was misnamed—that instead of urine he slung around, it was more like blood, and he should be called Sergeant Slaughter or Blood Bath, or maybe Edgar Allan Poe, to match his macabre fetish. Then Uri cleared his throat and started clicking the end of his red pen, snapping me back to reality.

"As you can see, we have a lot of work to do on this memo." My mind wandered to NuPol. If he had not stopped coming in regularly, he would be addressing this—though in my heart, I knew that he would have pulled some stunt and made Uri upset, and it would have gotten back to me anyway. Uri must have seen that my mind was drifting because he leaned in and said, "Priority. We have to have a sense of urgency about these things." He enunciated each syllable in both "priority" and "urgency." I decided it was better not to point out that if there really was a sense of urgency, cutting him out of the review cycle would make sense.

I let out a bored exhale, much louder than I meant to, and decided to engage. Even a warrior turned general has to get his hands dirty occasionally. "Okay, what's the problem?"

Uri smiled. The bloody memo was his stage, and my invitation opened the curtain. He would get to belittle me and my staff, make us jump through hoops to redo this memo, and then later find problems and have us put it back the way it was to begin with. He played his part well.

"I wish I could say there was just *a* problem, but there are several. The biggest one is at the beginning. Your guy, this NuPol, revised the title for the position."

"We were told to revise the title. Before, it was Assistant Sub-Secretary, but it was felt that someone could make a disrespectful acronym." Me, the warrior turned general, had shifted into "defend my troops" mode.

Uri put the memo on my desk and tapped it with the end of his still-open red pen, making pockmarks all over the subject line. "Look at it now."

My eyes drifted to the page and then drifted down. I saw that Uri had a point.

"That's right," he said with a smirk of satisfaction. "You don't think that would make a disrespectful acronym?" He kept tapping to make sure I didn't miss it.

Deputy Interim Chief. He continued.

"Yes, all somebody has to do is cleverly add a 'K' onto that, and it will be a disaster. Can you imagine how terrible this could be?" Uri was one for hyperbole.

I was so busy concentrating on my new position that I had failed to remind NuPol that I needed to review this before it went into the concurrence process.

"Okay," I conceded. "I'll have NuPol come up with a better title, not prone to mockery."

"Yes, and that needs to be done ASAP." The only thing Uri liked better than pointing out someone's mistakes was to then start bossing them around. "In fact, I think we need to have regular conference calls until this gets ironed out. Send me an invite." The only thing Uri liked better than bossing people around was to use their mistakes to make his own jobs program. These stupid calls will allow Uri to flourish in his three loves: pointing out mistakes, bossing us around, and making this his new jobs program.

"Okay, I'll get him moving on this today."

"The sooner the better. Like now," Uri barked, standing up. He started tapping his red pen against his chin like he was thinking about something. "I don't think I need to get the higher-ups involved just yet, but I'll let them know I'm handling this." He hadn't realized that he was tapping the wrong end of his open red pen against his face, and now he had red dots all over his chin and cheeks. He looked like one of those freckled Howdy Doody dolls I once saw in a vintage antique store in Old Town Alexandria. I cough-covered a laugh, thinking about how much I have had to do that lately. He looked at me strangely but turned to leave. On his way out, he grabbed the door, turned back to me, and reiterated, "Don't forget; set up meetings to discuss this. I expect to see a calendar invitation in my inbox when I get back to the office." His final command was meant to humiliate me, but I just stared at his dotted chin and cheeks. He gave one last smirk as he disappeared from my doorframe, and I had one last cough-covered laugh. I guess we both had our moment.

I called NuPol's extension and was surprised when he picked up the phone. He sauntered into my office, flopped down in the guest chair, slouched, and draped his arm over the back of the chair next to his. I was tempted to bark at him to straighten up to regain some of my dignity after the earlier embarrassment at the hands of Uri, but I knew he wouldn't. And even a new general knows that you don't bark commands unless you have a good response to the question, "Or else what?"—which I didn't.

I cleared my throat and sat forward in my chair to seize the commanding posture position. "We have a problem, NuPol."

His eyes drifted from looking out the window to looking at me, and then his head followed, turning owllike until he was facing me straight on. At that moment, I thought there was a fifty-fifty chance he was going to charge over the desk and knock me out of my chair. But he sat perfectly still, which was even more troubling. I tried to sit stoically but felt myself twitch.

"I had a chat with Uri this morning," I said, "and he found a major problem with the memo you have been working on."

He let out a sarcastic half laugh at the name Uri. "You mean the memo I was fixing because you screwed it up?"

I decided to turn the other cheek on this comment, or else this brief counseling session could turn into an all-day discussion. I knew NuPol's techniques better than anyone but was in no better shape to outmaneuver him.

"The new title you chose for the position can be, uh, manipulated and interpreted negatively. We can't have people mocking our senior management." I regretted the words as soon as I said them. I wish I'd had time to rehearse how I was going to assign him the simple task of coming up with a new title, but his quick appearance in my office had thrown me off. Instead, I had instinctively regurgitated a similar version of the words Uri had vomited on me, which I had passively accepted, but NuPol never would.

He slowly straightened up and leaned forward in the chair, lowering his head slightly while keeping his eyes on mine. He was like a big cat in the jungle getting ready to pounce. This series of moves and the silence for a few seconds that followed were even more menacing than his earlier owl-head move. I wanted out of there.

"Do you hear yourself, Ace? You have become pathetic. You used to laugh at stupid remarks like that, and now you are making them. Do you realize how much you have degraded in the short time you've been Acting Director? And now you are bothering *me* with something trivial like this?"

For a minute, the general had turned to warrior again. "NuPol, I am not asking you to shake heaven and Earth. I'm asking you to come up with a new title and update the memo, that's all."

At this, NuPol rose out of his chair and hunched over, resting on his clenched fists on my desk. "Our senior management is deserving of nothing but mocking, and the old Ace would know that. I can't believe you are letting Uri boss you around. I never thought it would happen to you. Just run this up the chain as it is, bypass Piss Pants, and show some balls for once."

I decided to rise out of my seat slowly and mirror his position, hunching over the desk and resting on my clinched fists, which kind of hurt, though I didn't let it show. "NuPol, this is not about who is bossing who around. It is about what's in the best interest of the agency. We both need to care about that."

NuPol kept his position but turned his head toward the window and started shaking it in an "I don't believe what I'm hearing" way. I decided the best thing to do was to lower the temperature and speak calmly.

"NuPol, we've been friends a long time. I know it's awkward having me here giving you assignments. Believe me, I didn't want this, but now that I've been asked to do it, I want to do a good job. Can't you at least cooperate with me a little for the sake of our friendship?"

NuPol turned his head back to me, quickly this time, like a mousetrap that had snapped. "As long as you are in this position, we are not friends. Just remember that."

At this, he stood up straight and turned to leave.

I composed myself. "Uh, let me know if you want to brainstorm ideas for titles." Without turning around to face me, he dropped his head and mumbled something I didn't understand. He took a step toward the door, and I lightly slapped the desk, which caused him to stop. "You forgot this," I said nicely but firmly as I picked up the folder with the memo that Uri had left me. He turned around and jerked it out of my hand. He walked out mumbling something again that sounded like "ass," but I couldn't be sure.

I sat back down and dropped my head for a moment. Gone was both the warrior and the general. On pause for the moment was my satisfaction at implementing my legacy. I felt alone. I had lost my friend just because I asked him to do his job. I was only trying to do the right thing, but it seemed like everybody hated me. The people on staff who were previously indifferent to me, like Negativa Diva and Mini, hated me, NuPol hated me, Buzz was strangely absent, and Uri was bossing me around. I wondered how Less did it. I knew he wasn't happy, but he seemed to hold everything together somehow.

I stood up to go to the restroom and accidentally bumped the desk. I heard a *clink* that I had not heard before, and a small key with clear tape that had apparently been on the underside of the desk fell onto the floor. I stood staring at it for a moment and then looked toward the door and then back to the fallen key. I had a hunch, and I was right. The key fit the bottom desk drawer, and out of curiosity, I turned the key and opened it.

I figured out one way Less held it together.

20

Meeting with More of Less and My Legacy: The Shared Drive, Part II (My Reward)

That afternoon, I heard a chime on my screen alerting me to the More of Less staff meeting. Finally, the one place where people still respected me for taking initiative and doing my job. After the day I had, this meeting couldn't come at a better time.

I slowly opened the door of my office enough to stick my head out to make sure the coast was clear. Looking from left to right, I saw nothing and darted toward the elevator. I was relieved that no one was in my path, not even Buzz wanting to give me an update on all he was doing, but I admit I was a little surprised. I went from having to avoid the gauntlet of staff to basically being left alone. Maybe they figured out that nagging me was not fruitful. There is a limited amount that anyone, even a supervisor, can do to make any of their situations better. I can do even less than Less because I am not actually their supervisor; I'm Acting.

Acting in our agency is kind of a no-man's-land for a supervisor. You have responsibility for what does and doesn't get done but no real authority to make it happen. When I mentioned this to Less in a conversation before he left, he gave me the old "use your persuasion" speech. But anyway, I was only an elevator ride, a walk through the basement corridor, and another elevator ride away from the one place where people understood what I was going through, where they still—dare I say—liked me. I was sure they thought I was bold in my vision to make this a better place by getting rid of the horrible shared drive. Who knows? I may even be an inspiration for them to take action in their own departments. It might be a brave new world in my agency, and it was all because of me.

I stood up a little straighter as I walked into More of Less's meeting. About half the staff was there, but More of Less had not arrived. I went to my chair and sat down, hoping he wouldn't embarrass me too much when he started praising me for my initiative.

More of Less was the last one to show up and had a stern look on his face. At the previous meetings, he'd looked indifferent, but today, he looked agitated. I honestly didn't know how he managed to ever look anything but upset, especially since his problems were compounded because he was at a higher level. The problems of everyone under him eventually rose to his level. He sat down, pulled his chair up to the table, and got down to business. He turned the meeting over to the Director of Events to share the good news that we are having an inspirational and motivational event next week, since it is the Month of Other Disadvantaged Employees and individuaLs. The earlier email that announced this fact to us had a note at the bottom that acknowledged how well the acronym fit and how thankful the agency was to the team that came up with MODEL Month. In fact, the team was getting an award from the Deputy Secretary for their creativity. I later found out the back story as to why the acronym used the "L" instead of the "I" in individual. It was because the "I" would spell out MODEI, and the "DEI" part would hit the BLOGE algorithm, and the initiative would be flagged for elimination until some judge delayed it, and then it would be tied up in court for months. I had to admit, for that bit of genius, this team really did deserve an award.

The Events Director explained that we were fortunate to be able to secure the time of a very important person to speak at the event. I had never heard of them, but they were the best-selling author of several books, a speaker at various federal agencies, a former ambassador, an activist, a community organizer, an expert witness at various discrimination trials, and an entrepreneur, having created several perfume and clothing lines. Their topic was discussing all the structural problems in society and how the system was rigged so that no one like them could ever succeed.

I made a note not to miss the event. The only remaining challenge the Director noted was that the speaker and their entourage had to stay at the Four Seasons in Georgetown because apparently the Willard Hotel, where we usually put up our guest speakers, did not have appropriate accommodations; that we needed to find bedsheets of a certain ply from a certain country southwest of Egypt and pillows made of a certain synthetic feather that had been produced by a startup at Stanford; and that our budget didn't account for these speaker necessities. More of Less said he would find the money somewhere, even if he had to cut something else, because this was so important. Everyone nodded, including me.

We then went around the table and gave our updates. I kept mine short and sweet to give More of Less time to praise me for my vision and courage in the quest for my legacy. I said that we were working on a memo to name the new position and that we were collaborating with Uri to make sure it was the right one to reflect the prestige of the position. More of Less seemed to wince when I mentioned Uri, but he just nodded and looked at the person beside me and said, "Next." I was a little surprised he didn't take the opportunity to praise me, but a short time later, I understood. After the last director gave their update, he wished everyone a good afternoon but then said, "Ace, I need you to stay."

Now it all made sense. He was going to praise me in private. That is best so the others didn't feel so inadequate. I felt a smile creep across my face as I said, "Gladly." Everyone left, and I picked up my notebook and moved to the chair at the other end of the table beside his as he got up to close the door.

I couldn't stop smiling. After all, this was to be the pinnacle of my short tenure as supervisor. It had started out bumpy, and I didn't know if my friendship with NuPol would recover, but I was aiming for a higher purpose: my legacy. I mentally rehearsed how I would respond when he heaped praise on me about my courage in taking on the shared drive. Maybe he would ask me to stay in the position permanently, even after Less came back. Part of me hated to do that to poor Less. I mean, after all, I knew we weren't an easy bunch to manage. In fact, the group of me, NuPol, Buzz, Mini, and especially Negativa Diva would cause any supervisor to wonder if they were cut out for this work.

Then a thought occurred to me. I wouldn't have to knock poor old Less out of the saddle at all. When I became the permanent supervisor of the group, I would make him my deputy. I would have him deal with the staff issues that I didn't want to. He was experienced at that, especially with NuPol. He would basically just keep on doing what he was doing before, and I would be left to form a strategic vision and lead the group. I could find us new work—work that excited everyone. I would make them do a personality survey and match everyone with their passions and purpose. Buzz could teach others how to properly express all the work they were doing, which I suspected was his dream job. I would even work on Negativa Diva. Maybe I could change her back to the enthusiastic, optimistic woman that I'm sure she was before the system beat her down.

I would stop resisting BLOGE, or whatever the efficiency gurus were calling themselves these days, and I would work with them to develop new processes and procedures, and we would be the model of productivity. Heck, I might carve out my own detail and go around to other agencies and show others how we moved from a department in the doldrums to one that inspired everyone. I would change our office, which in turn would change our agency, which in turn would change the entire federal government, which in turn would change the country and the whole world! And to think, it all started from my modest initiative to confront the shared drive.

"How is it going?" More of Less asked with a glare.

I understood that this was the small talk leading up to the big announcement about my new life.

"Oh, it's going well," I responded, hoping my enthusiasm wasn't too obvious. "Everyone seems to be working together, and I have submitted a proposal that I think will be a major initiative to completely address the problems we have had with the shared drive."

He rubbed his face and looked away from me. "Uh, they do seem to be working together, but not the way you think." He pulled out a brown case, removed a pair of small-framed reading glasses, and put them on the end of his nose. He opened the folder in front of him. "Seems like they are only working together to complain about you."

I felt my enthusiasm gush out like sand from a freshly stabbed burlap sack. "What? Uh, what do you mean?"

He looked at the paper he had just grabbed from the folder. "Ace is arbitrary and capricious. He lets some staff members get away with coming in late to work, avoids having critical conversations and coaching moments, and does not recognize important contributions from team members."

He laid down the paper and looked back at me. "I could go on, but you get the gist. It doesn't seem like anything is going well. There are thirty-seven complaints against you in this memo. HR was cc'd as well."

I knew this was a Negativa Diva thing, right down to using the words "coaching moment," like she would ever respond to anyone's coaching, let alone mine.

I put on my best "this is unfortunate but not as bad as it looks" tone. "Well, sir, I am sure I know who wrote that, and it is a disgruntled employee, and she, I mean they, are always unhappy."

He glanced down at the paper again and then at me for what I'm sure was effect. "They all signed it, not just one person. Seems you are very unpopular with your staff."

My façade was gone, and I inadvertently mumbled what I was thinking. "Even NuPol?"

Then his expression turned, and his glare left. "Oh, NuPol,

that's right, I forgot he was in your group. For some reason, I thought he worked for the lawyers. God knows he keeps them busy enough. No, he didn't sign the letter. I guess at least he is happy."

My guard was down, and I felt my anger mixed with hurt swell like the federal debt. I couldn't hold it in any longer. "He isn't happy. Nobody is. I just had an argument with him before I came over about a memo he is working on. I seem to have annoyed everyone on my staff without trying."

More of Less looked toward the window and away from me. "Well, normally, I would say that's a good thing, but in this case, you have managed to not only annoy them but piss them off. But you mentioned the memo. There is some good news there. It came into the concurrence queue today, and from what I understand, it looks like it's ready. Executive Secretariat needs to run it by one other person, but once it gets this far, it should be good to go."

"That *is* good news. At least something is going well," I managed to get out, although I was really thinking that NuPol should have worked with me on the new title. But I would take that one piece of good news and focus on the outcome instead of the process problems. That was actually two wins: The memo and my legacy.

"Uh, the other matter is about your proposal, as you call it, to fix the shared drive. Ace, the shared drive is set up the way it is for a reason, and that is to allow us to collaborate better. You see, without the shared drive, everyone does things their own way, and it's kind of like the Wild West," he said, holding up his index fingers and clicking his thumbs to have a "bang, bang" effect. "We like to work together here, and besides, the shared drive helps employ some of our people with maintenance and upgrades. There is no need to mess with it."

I could hardly contain a laugh, but as I was getting ready to unload on both him and the shared drive, he grabbed another piece of paper and handed it to me.

"I had to write up a reprimand for you. I'll let you read it when you get back to your office, but basically, it says that your effort to change the shared drive and instead have everyone work in their individual drives demonstrates that you have challenges with collaboration and need to be put on a performance improvement plan, specifically regarding working with others. It seems the people in your department do that better than you do." He waited for a minute, I assume for me to respond, but I didn't. Then he added, "But I did you a favor. I alluded to the complaint letter from your staff, but I didn't include the specifics here. I think that would have put it over the top, resulting in your suspension, especially since the efficiency folks may be looking for more heads to roll once we get beyond the current court order delaying their latest push."

I took the paper in my shaking hands and only managed to whisper an "Okay." Then I looked up as I felt water collecting in my eyes that I hoped wouldn't show. More of Less started to look blurry to me. "Any advice for me on how to proceed until Less gets back?"

His eyes drifted up as if he was thinking and searching for an answer on the ceiling. "Well, why don't you look at how Less handled situations. I mean, he wasn't perfect, but at least he figured out how to survive. Study how he responded and what he did and didn't do in situations. You have access to his emails, right?"

I felt my eyes widen. "No, I don't think they ever set me up with that."

"Well, as an acting supervisor, you are entitled to access those, since you are picking up where he left off. Get with IT and get those emails. I'll send them a message when I get back to my office and approve it. Who knows? It might help."

More of Less rose up and started walking toward the door. When I didn't move, I heard him say, "I think there's another meeting in here shortly." I put my hands on the table and pushed myself up slowly. I'm sure it looked like I was doing a yoga pose. When I got to the door, he put his hand on my shoulder. "Look, Ace, you need to understand when you are empowered to fix a system and when you are meant to just become part of it. It's a mistake a lot of first-time supervisors make."

I nodded.

Then he sniffed in my direction. "Do you use the same after-shave as Less?"

I backed away and shook my head.

I walked like a zombie back to my office. I had made the ulti-mate mistake: I trusted my people. They hated me, management hated me, and I'm sure IT hated me because I had messed with their beloved shared drive. I understood now why nobody had been waiting to talk to me when I got off the elevator. They had been too busy stabbing me in the back. I'm sure they didn't know that More of Less was going to have this talk with me or at least Nega-tiva Diva and Mini would be waiting to see me with schadenfreude (appropriate word of the day this morning). But I received a small gift in that no one was waiting for me.

I slinked slowly back to my office, sure that I felt eyes behind me but not turning around to confirm. I forcefully closed the door and flopped down in my chair. The warrior turned general had fallen off the chariot and was lying like a mangled blob on the road waiting for the lions to come.

21

Mangled Blob and Comeback Strategy

That evening, I came straight from the bus station and collapsed on the couch, not even having energy to muster the last ten steps to the bedroom. Reima came out of the bedroom adjusting an earring. She looked nicely dressed up with her flowered sleeveless shirt, dark jeans, and white high heels. Her black hair, which she usually wore pulled back in a ponytail, lay playfully on her shoulders like tranquil waves in the ocean at sunset. Her shirt was showing just a whiff of cleavage, subtly whispering of the perfection underneath. My momentary pause to admire the beauty of the one I'd met all those years ago in college at the international party—the beauty with the red miniskirt and dangling black earrings who looked like a supermodel that I could not believe was looking at me, the one who has been my rock all these years and for whom I should be thankful for no matter what is going on at work—was quickly replaced by fear that I had forgotten some commitment to take her out to a nice place tonight. I will do most anything to make her happy, but there was no way I was going out tonight. I only had the energy to lie on the couch and think about how terrible my tenure as a boss has been.

My life tonight was going to consist of rising from the couch, maybe stopping by the bathroom, and collapsing into bed. I didn't want to share my misfortunes with her. I sensed she was actually proud that I had risen from a low-level bureaucrat to a supervisor. I'm sure she pictured me sitting in meetings plotting strategy, laying out milestones for projects, hobnobbing with upper management, slapping them on the back and telling jokes, and making the occasional trip to the White House and Congress to brief them on all our important initiatives. I overheard her a couple of nights ago talking to her sister and heard my name, then a bunch of Spanish, then the word "promotion," and I saw her smile. If only she knew how unimpressive the job was and how very unimpressively I had been doing it.

She held out her hand, fist closed, and I mustered the strength to lift my arm and held my hand under hers, open and palm up. It was the same way Less had presented me with the Beaker key. She unclenched her fist, and down fell a thin chain with her locket that had a picture of her mother. She turned her back to me, saying nothing, but this was a signal for me to get up and help unclasp the link and then put it on her. I usually made a joke about how small the clasp was and how it was harder than threading a needle with yarn. I didn't move, except to close my fist to secure the locket.

"Remember, I'm going out with las mujeres tonight." I still didn't move, and she turned her head to look over her shoulder at me. "You do remember, don't you? I've been telling you for weeks."

I normally would have engaged in a bit of banter about how messages of her whereabouts are always diluted with so much other information that I don't really grasp or remember the nuggets. But instead, I felt nothing but relief that I was not included. Las mujeres are her Latina friends, and all of them are married to white guys (gringos) like me. All the husbands are Americans except one guy who is German, and he's close enough. The women usually go by themselves, but when they occasionally let us tag along, they enjoy talking in front of us about all the stupid things their gringo husbands do. I can only imagine how they chew us up when we're not there, but it's all in good fun and always ends with a kiss and some version of "I wouldn't trade him for anything." At least I think that's what they are saying. I only know a few words, so it could be something more like, "I would trade him for anything else if I could." I prefer to assume the former; that's part of the magic of our marriage. I live in ignorance and assume anything she says about me in Spanish is good.

I tried to learn Spanish when we first got married, but it didn't take. I now know that I don't have the gift for languages. I only learn Spanish when I make her mad, and those aren't words I can use in front of las mujeres. I tried again when we moved to DC. I took classes at the Department of Agriculture, which has classes for about everything, but when they switched from reading and writing (which I managed at the basic level) to watching soap operas (which I didn't understand), it was the beginning of the end. I only learned two things watching the soap operas: I don't learn by listening, and they yell a lot in Latin American soap operas. When Reima asked me what I'd learned, I started yelling even louder than her, speaking what I'm sure was a nonsensical language, and afterward, she forbade me from ever taking another class or trying to speak Spanish again.

But it's not been bad. We have come through a lot, including having to leave a place we both loved. After college, I'd gotten a job as a consultant in a nice suburb of St. Louis, called St. Charles, and we got married. Every evening, we walked on the brick streets beside the river that flowed through town, talking about nothing, which meant everything. We had each other, and that is all that mattered. We wanted to stay forever and build a life there.

She was still waiting for her authorization to work when I got the devastating news one Friday afternoon that I was included in a round of layoffs. I tried to get a job so we could stay in the area, even interviewing for jobs I would never have applied for under different circumstances, but the local economy was bad, and there was no choice but to move. We'd had to wait nine years for her to get an interview to become a citizen. So much for the idiots who think that when you marry an American citizen, you automatically become a citizen. I used to be one of those idiots, but not anymore. I'm proud to say I'm a different kind of idiot now.

As tired as I was, I assumed the least I could do was to help her with the necklace. So I rolled off the couch, landing with a thud on the carpet on my hands and knees, though I didn't feel anything. She looked back over her shoulder where I had been lying on the couch, and I gathered the strength to pop up behind her.

"I don't know how women do this if they're by themselves," I reflected out loud as the clasp kept slipping in my thumb before I locked it into place.

"We have to do a lot of things ourselves. I'm not really sure what we need you for," she said teasingly.

"I agree," I said seriously, not meaning to say it out loud. She seemed to let out a quiet "huh," but I ignored it. "There." I was prouder than I should have been for my only accomplishment that day.

She turned around, and a serious look came across her face. "Are you okay, mi amor?"

I contemplated telling her about my day but decided not to ruin her evening. Usually, the incompetent gringo husband banter was in good fun, but today I could give her something to really be ashamed of.

"I'm just tired."

"Not easy being the boss, is it?" she replied and smiled.

"Not today," I responded. Then, with the last bit of strength I could muster, I grabbed her shoulders tenderly and leaned in, meeting her soft, painted lips with mine, working my tongue into the small opening between her teeth, which opened further, and meeting her tongue, which started rotating with mine.

"Wow, that was a surprise," she said, breathy as I smiled and then fell back onto the couch like struggling fish dropped into the bow of a boat.

The next day, I felt like I was carrying weights on my back and a dark cloud above. Once again, I got the small gift that no one was waiting for me when I got off the elevator. Maybe they were huddled in one of their cubes constructing their next complaint letter against me. I shuffled to my office, hearing my feet scoot, too tired to pick them up properly, pretending to look at my phone so others would think I was too busy to talk. Once inside my office, I remembered that this morning was our staff meeting, and the last thing in the world I wanted to do was face my staff. I re-sent the invite and penned a cryptic excuse. "Prior commitments, meeting overcome by events. Canceling today, will reschedule."

I realized that hiding in my office was only going to make me more depressed, so I decided to head over to the cafeteria. I had my phone in hand in case someone accosted me on the way to the elevator. I was almost home free when who should brush by me, clipping my elbow and stepping onto the elevator in front of me, but NuPol.

I stepped in after him and cleared my throat. "Good morning."

He looked at me and half laughed. It was a torturous ride on the way down. It seemed to take several minutes between floors; then I got an idea. Just before the *ding* sounded for the basement, I hit the stop button, and the elevator jerked. We both almost fell down, and NuPol said, "What the ef—?" not finishing his thought.

I took a breath. "Look, NuPol. We already talked about this. I didn't ask for this, and I don't want this. You want to control everything anyway, so I delegate the supervisor's position to you. I can do that, even if I'm Acting. Now you are in charge. You can do whatever you want."

He smiled and said, "Okay, I accept. Now I delegate it back to you. We can do this all day, and you know I'll win."

"Why don't you want it, NuPol? You have always wanted to be in charge. Now you can be."

NuPol pulled the button out to start the elevator again. "I am in charge, and you know I always do what I want. Accepting this will be a demotion. I control things more where I am than I ever could with any so-called position."

The elevator dinged, and he hopped off, but not before putting his hands on the door edges, sticking his face between the opening, and saying in a Jack Nicholson voice, "Heeeeere's NuPol!" He moved back, and the doors closed while both the elevator and I stood still, my own blurry face showing in the dingy silver door. I sighed and then pressed the button to open it.

The cafeteria was pretty empty this time of the morning. I went to the coffee line and got some Southern Pecan coffee, a strange exotic indulgence I enjoy in this federal café, where most food and beverage choices are middle-of-the-road and boring. I slipped my credit card in the slot and smiled at the cashier who never smiles back and only points to the machine when my card has cleared. It was kind of odd coming here without NuPol, but those days were over, and I needed to get used to it. I grabbed a table on the side of the large space. There were plenty of empty tables in the middle, but I really wanted to blend into the wall anonymously so I didn't have to interact with anyone. I had never felt this low at work, so I grasped for any small comfort. While I couldn't have my friend to share coffee with, at least I could still have coffee.

My mind was lost in reflections of the past two days, and I slurped a little louder than I intended, looking around to see if anyone of the meager group of people on this side of the room heard it. I scanned side to side but only saw a few other souls in suits and pant suits mindlessly looking ahead and sip-slurping— likely others who had once been brave warriors or even generals who were now reduced to blobs like me.

Then, a few tables down, I saw something that froze my head mid-turn and stopped my arm mid-raise. There she was: the woman who was the head of PR who attended More of Less's meetings. I thought about looking the other way and pretending I didn't see her, but if she saw me, she didn't acknowledge it. She was sitting alone, and I noticed that her hair was a bit unkempt, her curls dangling, and she didn't seem to have makeup on. She also seemed to stare down at the table in front of her. Her sleeveless blue shirt stood out among the small sea of jackets that the few others in the room were wearing. She had no jewelry, though I had noticed during Acronopoly that she had three or four gold and silver bracelets on each arm that appeared from underneath her jacket sleeves when she leaned forward and rested her elbows on the table. She looked less put together than she was in the meetings. I almost didn't recognize her, but my frozen gaze confirmed it really was her.

I was in no mood to network, but she did have one valuable piece of information that I needed, and I didn't know when I would get another chance to chat. I put down my disposable cup still full of coffee and walked over to her table.

"Uh, excuse me. I don't mean to bother you, but aren't you the head of PR?"

The woman slowly raised her eyes from the table and locked with mine, forcing out a suspicious, "Uh-huh." I could tell this was a "don't bother me" response, but I had one shot, and I was going for it.

"I'm Ace, and I'm acting for Less while he is in training."

She wrinkled her forehead and started nodding, rocking slowly with her upper body rather than nodding with her head in affirmation. "Oh, yes, you sit at the end of the table."

This time, I nodded and smiled. She'd acknowledged me. I was not at her end of the table, but at least she could see the area where I sat (a few feet and a world away from her).

"I wanted to congratulate you," I finally managed to say.

I sensed her comfort with me increasing as she leaned back in her chair and took a sip. She grabbed the string hugging the side of her cup and pulled the tea bag out, setting it on a folded napkin. "Congratulate me for what?" she asked between half sips. (Note here: sips, not slurps. I doubt she ever slurped in her life.)

"You won that ping-pong match with the acronyms in the meeting. It was kind of beautiful watching you work."

She put down her cup, and an actual smile appeared as she looked in the distance. For a moment, I realized she really didn't need makeup and actually looked better and more natural. "Oh, that. Yes, I must say that was a moment of pride. I usually lose, but I was equipped that day." Then she looked down at the table as her smile gradually vanished.

"Are you feeling okay?" I asked.

"Not really. They're bringing somebody in to be the head of our group. They will be my new boss, so I might not even go to the meetings anymore. Without face time, I'll be in the dark, and everything will be coming through the filter of my new boss. The efficiency guru said it was a boost to our organization, but it's a demotion for me. Everything this BLOGE group does seems arbitrary; there is no way to predict what they want, let alone satisfy them." Then she cleared her throat and seemed to regain her composure. I think this was the first time I realized that other generals sometimes get knocked down too.

I could feel our chitchat coming to a close, but I had one last question. I looked around to see if anyone was looking at us before I tried to pry open the eternal secret. "I have to ask, what was that final acronym that you used? I have been able to identify all the others, but not the knockout punch. What does SLA stand for?"

Her broader smile returned for a second and then turned subtle, as if she were an ancient sage getting ready to impart wisdom for the ages. "That one, I made it up. It stands for Six-Letter Acronym."

"Ahhhhhh, well played," I said like a court jester who just found the key to the kingdom. "Thanks. I'll let you get back to your drink."

I turned to walk away, and she said, "Uh, Acting Less?"

I turned around to face her.

"Actually, it's an initialism, not an acronym," she added.

"Noted," I said, pointing to my head as if showing her where that knowledge was going. I knew that, but I thought I might as well give her this know-it-all moment. After all, she just gave me a weapon to hopefully launch a comeback, and some form started to return to this warrior blob.

22

The Penultimate and Ultimate Battles

As I returned to my office, I felt a little spring in my step. I was still glad when I stepped off the elevator and no one was there, but I wasn't fearful either. Although I wasn't back to my blissful ignorance baseline, I certainly felt better than when I had gone to the cafeteria earlier. But I kept thinking about how the staff had done me wrong. Sure, I understand that anyone who is the supervisor has a target on their back, but I didn't do anything bad to these people. I'd only been trying to help, and they'd still screwed me. My mood slowly started shifting from depressed to an odd mixture of disappointment and anger.

I was sitting in my office opening my messages when Buzz, the backstabber, apparently developed the nerve to appear at my door. I looked up, I'm sure with an irritated look on my face, and expected him to begin telling me all the things he was working on. Instead, he got to the point and said, "I just sent a request for a new training. It should be in your inbox. It's in Phoenix, and it is about organizational development. Hurry up and approve it so I can make travel arrangements."

His voice annoyed me, the request annoyed me, and the presumption that I must approve it on his timetable really annoyed me. All I could do was imagine him gathering with the others to launch a complaint against me. I was acting supervisor, so maybe I should start acting like it.

I looked back down at my screen while maintaining the same irritated look. "I'll look at your request and consider it, Buzz. Right now, I have other matters I need to address." I gazed up, and he looked like he'd just eaten something he was going to spit out.

"My requests are always approved as soon as I put them in," Buzz said. "It's just a formality." His voice sounded whiny on the last few words.

"It can't be a formality anymore," I said. "Regarding training, I have to consider the needs of the office and fairness to everyone else."

"But Ace, you should just follow precedent and approve my request. It's for the good of the agency. This has never been an issue before."

I'd had it. "Well, it's an issue now. I told you I will consider it, but I have more pressing matters. After all, there have been complaints about me, so I am changing the approval process moving forward." I threw the last part in to give my answer a "you brought this on yourself" feel.

"But—" he started.

"As part of this new process, I will need a cost-benefit analysis for this training and a report on how the training will benefit not only you but our organization and the agency in general. I need that on my desk by noon, or I will assume you don't want me to consider it further."

He gave a long exhale and turned to leave.

I added, "And Buzz, do the report on the shared drive. I understand it is the preferred method." I heard his footsteps slowly fading outside my door, and I imagined him contemplating if he could even do the assigned task. I knew I wouldn't receive anything from him today. I opened my inbox and saw his request at the top. I clicked on it, deleted it, and then went to the recycle bin and deleted it again, saying out loud "absolutely" when the system asked if I was sure.

I started to feel the outline of a general taking shape, though there were still parts of the warrior blob hanging on. I had hit Buzz where it hurt. I wasn't trying to hurt him, but I wasn't trying to help him either. Somewhere between asshole and doormat is a sweet spot, and I felt like I had found it. With no time to waste, I sent the invite for a staff meeting that afternoon. One down, three to go.

Two messages popped up in my email. I scanned them and only acted on the first one; the other could wait. It appeared that I now had access to Less's emails. Though I wasn't sure how much it would help, I started digging into them. I looked for my name at first to see if Less was sabotaging me but didn't find anything I didn't already know about. There were only a few that weren't blast emails to the whole staff. However, there were a lot about everyone else. Apparently, I had access not only to his emails but also to his private directory. Less had kept his walled off from everyone else and not mapped to the shared drive. I dug through those emails and started to see messages between him and other supervisors archived on his individual drive, not like the shared one we have to tolerate. Maybe that is what all the supervisors did: They exempted themselves from the stupid policies they made us follow. I'd always understood that rank has privileges, but now I saw that one of those privileges is hypocrisy.

I felt my eyes widen with every new revelation in the messages. Then I started looking in other subdirectories, and it was as if I had found a treasure map that would lead me to the secret of how people like Less, who I never thought was a bad guy, dealt with the likes of his staff. There were a lot of messages about how stupid all the recent so-called efficiency initiatives were, how they got rid of only the best performers, and how everybody left was scared to do anything. I could have been upset because that's all I was trying to tell Less during my performance appraisal that led to this journal and my disastrous attempt at community service. But most of all, I just felt vindicated.

A big part of what I found, which I am now sure was a coping mechanism, was how much he complained about his staff (pretty much everyone except me) with his fellow supervisors and how much they complained about their staffs to him. The messages were much worse than the ones that Negativa Diva found and read aloud when we first set up the shared drive. I saw a message about Negativa Diva, and he used words like "sociopath" and "miserable human being." But my favorite line was a very lucid characterization of Negativa Diva in an exchange between Less and the HR Director. I kind of thought that this sort of thing was off limits, that you never shared your true feelings with HR or Legal. But apparently, I was wrong.

"Even with copious amounts of both therapy and medication, Negativa Diva will never be a decent human being, let alone an asset to the organization. I am thinking about requiring her to do a 360-degree analysis so she gets everyone's perspective of her. I hope it makes her cry and get sick so she will take a few days off. All I can do is marginalize her, work around her, and hope she gets tired and decides to leave, at which point I will give her a glowing recommendation so she can be someone else's problem."

His message was spot on. I never thought Less saw it as clearly as NuPol and I did. But Less didn't stop there; he also went into an analysis of Mini, though he had given her a different name: Broad Bottom (BB). He recognized the drama triangle at play just like we did.

"The only person I have less respect for than Negativa Diva is her sycophant, BB. Negativa could say squat, and BB would say, 'Where at?' She is an even more disgusting person because she has become subservient to the second most disgusting person. She has no core. Her only core is that she feels she must be loyal to Negativa, even if she ruins her relationships with everyone else in the process. I am her boss, and Negativa is on BB's same level, but BB is apparently too dense to know that. She is a coward, and she is too stupid to realize that Negativa has played her Rescuer in the Drama Triangle, where she has convinced BB that she is the Victim and I am the Oppressor. Even worse, she couples her loyalty to Negativa with an extreme level of stupidity. One time, I reminded the staff to turn in their financial interest forms, which everyone has to do, and BB forwarded the message to Negativa, stating that she would wait for further instructions on how to respond to 'our clueless boss.' And get this: She accidentally sent it to me. What a moron. I must say, BB is the only person more useless to me than Negativa. At least Negativa shows leadership by leading the idiot BB."

He also went off on Buzz and how he was always bothering everyone, talking about how much he does, though it never results in anything except more trainings. Less admitted that he sent Buzz to those without hesitation to get him out of the office. He had thousands of messages in the subdirectory named NuPol, which I didn't get a chance to dig into. I was sweating even reading this unfiltered, borderline cruel—but I admit accurate—assessment of his staff. But I still wondered, even with the venting in these messages, how did he handle all this without quitting? He couldn't deny the problems with his staff, which surely made it that much harder.

Then I came upon the subdirectory named "Miscellaneous" and realized I had found another potent coping mechanism. Some of the messages and draft documents there were very recent, even since Less went to training, which meant he was still saving messages there. I became paranoid that if he was copying messages there real time, maybe he could see me opening up his other emails. Though I had permission from More of Less, I still felt uncomfortable, so I decided to stop surfing his messages, at least for now. As I stood up, I accidentally bumped the desk and heard a *clink*, which reminded me of another coping mechanism.

The staff were all sitting around the table when I walked into the room. For the first time, I knew it was *my* meeting. I sat at the head of the ten-by-five-foot old gray army surplus table. There was mumbling when I walked into the room, but I was not there to listen. I was there to oppose anything anyone said and control the meeting. There was still a little bit of the blob left in me, but the outlines of the general were becoming less fuzzy. I had arrived.

"Okay, let's get to it. This is going to be efficient. Let's go around the table, and you have one minute to tell me what you are working on and if you need something from someone else in this room."

Negativa Diva cleared her throat, and, of course, her voice came out of Mini's mouth. "Uh, Ace, you forgot to go around the table and ask our pronouns."

I was ready for this. I didn't know what they would complain about first, but whatever it was, I was going to argue. I have nothing against pronouns, and someone can call themselves whatever they choose, but I knew that if I gave in at this point, the staff would take over, and I was not going to let that happen.

I put down my pen and folded my hands in front of me. "Mini, when was the last time we ever used pronouns in this meeting?"

She was not used to being challenged on something so controversial. Even Less would have caved and gone around the table, allowing them to hijack the discussion. But not me, not today. "Uh . . ." She looked at Negativa Diva, who didn't speak but glared at me.

I pounced. "Don't look at her. Look at me, and answer my question," I said sternly as I felt my eyebrows rise.

"I don't remember," Mini said, looking down at the table.

"If it comes up in this one, we'll revisit it, but there is no need to now. And by the way, that's your minute. Next."

I heard a gasp from Buzz, and NuPol started looking around the room. He seemed to be studying everyone.

I was feeling more empowered. "Okay, Buzz, you have one minute."

Buzz had been slowly scooting back in his seat and hiding behind NuPol but now shifted and leaned forward. "Well, the big thing I am working on is getting more training. I sent you the approval form."

I nodded slowly and said, "Yes, we discussed that. As I mentioned earlier, I am expecting some justification documents before we can move forward."

"But I never had to do that before," Buzz said in a whiny voice.

Without hesitating, I replied, "And your point is?"

Buzz started scooting back in his seat and hiding behind NuPol again.

I stared at the space where he was for a few seconds and then turned my eyes to NuPol.

"Mr. NuPol?" I said. "Your turn."

NuPol sounded almost timid, which I had never heard. "I submitted the memo that I have been working on with the title for the new position they created in Public Relations. It's a Senior Executive position." I did a slow nod for a few seconds and then spoke. "Yes, that is actually one of the success stories for our group. I understand they are getting ready to issue it."

Now was the moment I had dreaded, though I was prepared. It was still Negativa Diva, after all.

"Okay, Negativa Diva. You have one minute."

Her glare didn't change, and the crevice in her scowled face opened slowly. I knew it was on.

"I don't like the tone of this whole meeting."

In the past, I would have been intimidated, looked down at the table in front of me, and prayed that nobody saw or called on me. But not today, not the new me, and not now.

I looked at my watch in a smart-assed move. "Your minute is ticking away," I said in what I intended to be a condescending voice.

"I refuse to participate in this farce anymore."

I kept my tone calm. "This is the way it is going to be from now on, and as a team member, you will participate."

"I am not to be treated this way. I don't like your tone, and I don't like you."

Now I felt a smirk on my face. "You have made that clear, and frankly, my dear Negativa, I don't give a damn."

She slammed her meaty paw on the table. "You are swearing in our meeting! I am going above you to complain."

"Again?" I asked. Then I went in for the kill. "You know that with the second complaint you have to submit an SLA within an hour of the supposed offense, don't you? Do you have an SLA prepared already?"

She sat silently for a few seconds, and then I raised my voice slightly. "Negativa, *do you have an SLA prepared already?*"

Out of the corner of my eye, I could see NuPol's eyes widen. I saw Mini look at her master's face with an "I need this" look. In the pregnant moments between when I asked the question and Negativa finally taking a breath, Mini's eyes drifted down to the floor as her whole world shattered.

"Ne-ga-tiv-a," I sang in a singsong voice, when she suddenly shot back, "No!"

"That's what I thought," I said, sinking the knife deeper. "Then obviously your complaint is unserious and should go no further. Your minute is up, and the meeting is over."

I stood up, surveying the battlefield and the wounded bodies lying around. NuPol was the only one who still seemed to be alive and kicking, though he had a terribly confused look on his face. I went to my office and slammed the door. This was the best I had felt since I took on this horrid assignment. This was even better than if I had achieved my legacy and killed the shared drive. I had taken everyone down, everyone except NuPol, and his time would come soon. I had to lie (I prefer to say bluff) about the policy of submitting a second complaint, obviously, since an SLA did not exist. But I knew Negativa Diva would never admit that she didn't know something. I also knew the lie would keep her occupied, looking for a nonexistent requirement for days, maybe weeks. By the time she learned the truth and went forward with a second complaint, I wouldn't be in the position anymore. For the first time, I had a feeling she would be looking for it by herself; Mini's impression of her had been destroyed. Mini might have to finally grow up and stop worshipping Negativa Diva.

And Buzz had been humbled because someone had finally told him no.

I picked up the phone and called Reima. I was leaving early, and we were heading out to Middleburg to hit a winery that stayed open late and get an awesome meal at her favorite restaurant at the Red Fox Inn.

The general was back, if only for a few more days.

23

The Beginning of the End

The rest of that week was rather pleasant. When I arrived in the morning, no one was waiting as I stepped off the elevator. Buzz, Mini, and especially Negativa Diva avoided me like an unmasked Covid cougher. NuPol had returned to his practice of coming in late, but now the staff didn't care that I didn't care.

The only real break in the cadence of the week was More of Less's meeting that Thursday. I enjoyed the elevator ride and walk to it, and I even heard myself whistling "Funkytown" without even thinking about it.

The meeting was more entertaining and less cordial this time, and the PR and Events Directors got into a heated discussion. I was rooting for the PR Director, since she gave me the secret of SLA. Whatever one said the other would oppose simply because the other one said it. This latest argument was about how high-level events with dignitaries should be handled, and it seemed they were both territorial about it. The PR Director seemed to be the aggressor, probably because she—like me—knew her time was limited. What started as a general discussion about putting on events accelerated to a personal attack, and More of Less seemed loath to intervene. After some discussion, the rapid fire came. I was slightly disappointed at the lack of acronyms or initialisms, but the battle was still quite the spectacle.

Events: "This is our lane, and we are developing procedures to improve. We know what we're doing."

PR: "Show me the procedure. The last few events have not gone well."

Events: "We are reviewing our procedures to determine how we can improve."

PR: "Procedures, procedures. Why doesn't your staff just do it right?"

Events: "We *are* doing it right. We are data driven and looking at our practices. We are also planning to survey other agencies to benchmark our processes and practices."

PR: "You always hide behind processes and surveys. I bet your staff can't tie their shoes without a procedure."

(Voices start getting louder at this point.)

Events (leaning forward): "We can tie our shoes fine. You just don't understand anything about being data driven and evidence based."

PR (leaning forward and mirroring the position): "Blah, blah, blah. You could be assigned to tie your shoes, and you'd set up such a bureaucracy that nobody could ever tie their shoes again."

Events: "What is it about you and shoes? Your heels don't even have shoelaces."

PR: "I'm hearing blah, blah, blah, but my shoes are still untied."

Events: "Your shoes don't tie."

PR: "I'm sure you need to conduct a survey on how everyone else in government ties their shoes."

Events: "You hate best practices."

PR: "My shoes are still untied."

At this, More of Less couldn't take it anymore and decided to jump in. "We're out of time, so let's take this discussion offline."

I went to the cafeteria after the meeting for a cup of Southern Pecan coffee. I sat at the same table as the week before. I was hoping the head of PR would come in so I could congratulate her on her second victory, but apparently, she had to stay after school, so to speak. She didn't score a knockout this time, but I definitely thought she was ahead on points.

I was sipping and reflecting when who should come and sit down in front of me but NuPol. So now it was time: me versus NuPol. He had brought down entire general counsel offices and was probably the reason that Less was sent to training. He was my one piece of unfinished business.

"That was some meeting you had," NuPol said, his tone such that I couldn't tell if it was a compliment, an insult, or a setup.

I sat my cup down on the off-white particleboard table between us. "Well, I tried to make it *efficient*. That's the word of the day."

"You seem to be stepping into this role," he replied, which sounded like a compliment. His voice had its usual raspy tone that had annoyed me during our recent discussions, but somehow, it was a touch more endearing today, like old times.

"I'm trying to do my best, even if I'm just the temporary supervisor. I tried to be a nice guy, and all that got me was a group complaint. Apparently, you didn't get the chance to sign it too. I guess you were late that day." I had dispensed with the niceties and fired the first shot.

NuPol leaned forward in his seat and folded his hands in front of me. "Ace, I did have a chance, and I was pushed by all three of them. They even offered to take out the part about one of the employees being late if I would fold. I knew that was me. But I didn't sign."

This disarmed me. Maybe there was still a remnant of our friendship, despite our uncomfortable recent interactions.

"I guess I should thank you for that," I said sincerely, but still guarded.

NuPol looked to the side. "I'm not going to say you have done well, because you are still in a position of authority, and I never say nice things about those in authority." He paused for a minute and then looked at me. "But I'm not going to insult you either. I'll just say you could have been worse."

With that, he pushed himself up from the table and started to walk away, stopping once to give me a look that was somewhere between expressionless and a forced quarter smile. I couldn't tell which, and it didn't matter. I looked down at my cup and watched the coffee lazily swirl as I slowly moved my hand in a circular motion. I felt a half smile creep onto my own face. I reflected for a moment on my relationship with my friend. NuPol had not been happy about my tenure, but at least he hadn't pulled some of the same stunts he did with Less, disrupting meetings and declaring his disorders, which he never had to prove and I always assumed were mostly BS and just meant to cause Less headaches. At least he had held back a little and also didn't sign the complaint. NuPol and I would be okay. Even my sabbatical as a supervisor had not destroyed our friendship.

I went back to get a second cup of coffee and bumped into a guy I had seen at an awards ceremony at another agency. "Excuse me," I said and glanced at the name on his visitor's badge: Jon Barrett. He had done something like an investigation at a chemical plant. He smiled and seemed nice, but I didn't want to get caught in a conversation. I took my coffee back to the office to get caught up on some messages and get ready for the final task of the week.

On Friday afternoon, I addressed the other message I had received earlier in the week. I started typing: "Please note that Less is returning on Monday. Let's all welcome him back, and I ask that you show him the same respect that you have shown me. Ace."

I opened the bottom desk drawer, and after exercising Less's (now my) coping mechanism, I hit Send and bolted to the elevator. No more conversations this week, or ever, as a supervisor.

24

The End of the End

I came in early on Monday morning as a courtesy to Less so we could chat before the others arrived. Less was already in the office, sitting at his desk, his hair mussed up and the top button of his shirt undone.

"They let you go early," I said. "You didn't have to stay the whole three months."

"Yes, the training was cut short. Apparently, all our complaints about the new efficiency measures were making the facilitators uncomfortable, and they got word back from our upper management that we should stop the training. My guess is they figured out that putting problematic supervisors together was not a good thing since we learn from each other. How were things here?"

"I thought it was going okay, but then I got a complaint letter filed against me, from everyone but NuPol."

"Just one letter?" he said in a questioning tone. "You must have done pretty well."

"Well, I tried to be nice and they complained, so I became a jerk, denied Buzz training, and shut Negativa Diva down in a meeting, which automatically shut down Mini, of course."

Less chuckled. "I should have done that years ago. The stupid training I just had kept saying it's the supervisor's fault if there are problems in the office—that everyone can be motivated to work well and that it is our job to find what motivates them and support and coach them. Blah, blah, blah. What a pile of horseshit. I knew at that point the training facilitators had never managed anyone in the federal government, or probably anywhere. By the way, Ace, a little trick I picked up years ago is that if you ever wonder how you've done, look at it objectively, as if you are someone else. Even talking about your actions in third person helps. I know it sounds weird, but you might realize you had good reasons for doing what you did."

I felt the need to compliment him. "You know, you already do pretty well, Less. You have a hard job. I guess I never knew how hard until now."

"Thanks, Ace. I'm glad you are on my staff. Speaking of which, I have an assignment for you. They caught something in the memo about the 'new' new title," he said with finger quotes on the first "new." He continued. "I think NuPol was working on it, and it slipped through some reviews, but Uri found something at the last minute. I guess we need to start over. Uri is bringing me his comments. You know he gets off on handing me papers with his red marks on them, kind of like a sadistic butcher. I'll bring them to you after he stops by."

"I can't wait," I said sarcastically, forcing out a laugh.

He stood up and reached out his hand to shake mine. "Thanks, Ace. Sounds like you did a good job, and I don't have too much to apologize for. That's my measure of success when I delegate."

As I reached out to shake his hand, I bumped his desk, and we heard the clink. We both looked down. I slowly met his gaze and cleared my throat. "Uh, you might need to refill your bourbon supply. I would, but don't know how to sneak it in."

He smiled. "Just say it's for a reception for the Secretary. Security never checks that."

I nodded at the new tip. "By the way, your boss thinks we use the same cologne. I don't think he knows."

Without pause, Less blurted out, "He's an idiot."

I hesitated to tell him the next part but decided that since we were sharing openly, I might as well tell all. "They gave me access to your files. Your boss thought that seeing how you respond and cope might help me deal with situations."

"He should have shown you the liquor instead," Less responded.

I smiled and continued. "It seemed to have your personal files too, like messages you drafted." He didn't respond, but I added, "By the way, My Chance, I have been a fan of yours on Nextdoor for a while."

He gave a half nod. "That helps too, as you probably already know. I'm sure you have figured out who my Nextdoor nemeses are, but if not, you will. Don't tell them." He mimicked a silent "oops" and put his finger to his lips in a hush gesture.

"That's just between you and me," I added with a wink.

I went back to my cubicle and saw Negativa Diva and Mini pass each other but not say a word. Neither acknowledged me. It would take time for Negativa Diva and Mini to adjust to their new reality. If anything, I had helped bring about the start of a new day. And I thought we would be all right in the end, because after all, we are a team. We could make it, even if the best we ever achieve is a sort of functional dysfunctionality.

I passed by NuPol's cubicle and started to step in, but his back was turned to me, and I could see that his screen was pulled up to Nextdoor. It was the same when I passed Negativa Diva's cubicle a little later during my coffee run. I also noticed that on both their desks were journals, just like the one the efficiency guru gave me. Are they having to do this penance too? It would be interesting to see their perspectives, if anyone should ever "find" their journals.

I got to my cubicle after my coffee run, sat down, and turned on my computer. Buzz knocked on the frame of my nonexistent door and stuck his head in. "Can I tell you what's going on?"

I swung around in my chair and slapped my thighs with both hands. "I'd love to hear what's going on, Buzz, but I have to work on a memo right now. You know the boss is back. Can you fill me in after lunch? I have the whole afternoon reserved for you."

He pointed at me with a "bang, bang" finger and smiled. "You got it."

Buzz and I would be okay.

I opened my inbox and had a gift inside. Apparently, Effing G had been put on leave because of some (I presume inappropriate) old tweets he had posted. Thus, all ongoing initiatives under his jurisdiction were now optional, which basically meant that my journal and community service requirements were canceled. I can stop keeping this journal, and I think I will, but I am glad I had it during this tough spot in my life. I texted Reima that I wanted to have Ethiopian for dinner, and she replied with a simple, "Si, mi amor."

I sat back in my chair and hooked my fingers behind my head. For the first time in a long time, I was thankful for my job. I was returning to my position, but I was not returning as the same person. Maybe I would take Less's advice and reflect as if I were someone else watching myself.

Ace had seen life at a higher level, and it was not better. The grass wasn't greener. He had changed; he was not the naïve bureaucrat he had been before, doing the job but wishing for something better. He wasn't going to complain about the efficiency crap either, which seemed to be petering out anyway.

Things weren't so bad. Ace had a friend in NuPol, he had entertainment with his other colleagues, and he had a good relationship with his supervisor. They'd even bonded over shared secrets.

Ace heard another knock on his cubicle frame, and Less appeared. "Here's the memo from Uri. It has a lot of red on it, but the biggest problem is the name: Public Relations Interim Chief. Can you imagine the crap we'll get if someone adds a 'K' to that acronym?"

Ace couldn't help but smile. This was NuPol's last gift to management during Ace's tenure, and it was now his problem to solve. "I'll come up with something else, Less."

Less started to walk away but turned around and said, "Go ahead and work in the shared drive."

"Sure thing." Ace couldn't deny it any longer. He was a changed man. Ace reached gleefully for his mouse to search the shared drive for the new format for memos and had one last reflection, sort of reminiscent of the ending of a book he'd read in high school.

Ace loved the shared drive.

About the Author

Stephen J. Wallace says he is a writer trapped in an engineer's body, or vice versa. His first novel, *Hazardous Lies*, received numerous recognitions and awards in the categories of mystery, thriller, or suspense, including the IBPA Benjamin Franklin Gold Award and the Readers' Favorite Gold Medal. It was also a winner of the NYC Big Book Award, the Independent Author Network Book of the Year Award, and the Reader Views Reviewers Choice Award, as well as a finalist for the Storytrade Book Awards and the Chanticleer International Book Awards. Stephen's short stories have appeared in the *Schuylkill Valley Journal*, the *Vita Poetica Journal*, and *The Mark Literary Review*. He has lived in the Washington, DC, area for several years with his wife, Madeleine, but occasionally visits his home state of Kentucky.

You can read more about Stephen and his work at
stephenjwallace.com.